Wes wanted more

He crushed Cara's body against his, the sensation both relief and torture.

She tore her mouth from his. "We have to stop. I don't do this with colleagues."

"Okay," he said, letting go of her and stepping back. Blood still roared in his head, but he forced his desire to chill.

Cara stared at him with a shocked, wide-eyed expression that reflected his own feelings. "I'm sorry. I don't know what got into me. Can we just forget it ever happened?" she continued. "We have to work together, and I need to concentrate on the case. Besides, I'm sure you have plenty of women lining up to..."

Wes leaned one shoulder against her front door. He smiled and brushed a strand of hair off her face. "But I was just about to let you cut to the front of the line."

"The *front* of the line? Aren't I lucky?"

His grin only widened. "Let me inside, and we could both get lucky."

Dear Reader,

Over the past few years I've developed a weakness for the Kimball family. They're a close, boisterous bunch, who support and challenge each other through all the bumps and heights in their lives. As I dived into Wes's life, I wondered how they would all react to a new kind of test—not just a romantic tangle, but a danger to the very life of their town.

An arsonist is loose in Baxter, and Wes, who longs for acceptance but still walks his own path, is called on to solve the mystery.

I enjoyed exploring Wes's strengths and vulnerabilities and watching him be awed, frustrated and, finally, embraced by love. By the time I finished the book, he and Cara felt like old friends. I hope they do the same for you.

Visit my Web site at www.wendyetherington.com and tell me what you think. Or you can still reach me via regular mail at P. O. Box 3016, Irmo, SC 29063.

Happy reading!

Wendy Etherington

Books by Wendy Etherington

HARLEQUIN TEMPTATION

944—PRIVATE LIES
958—ARE YOU LONESOME TONIGHT?

HARLEQUIN DUETS

76—MY PLACE OR YOURS?
93—CAN'T HELP FALLING IN LOVE
HUNKA HUNKA BURNIN' LOVE

WENDY ETHERINGTON

SPARKING HIS INTEREST

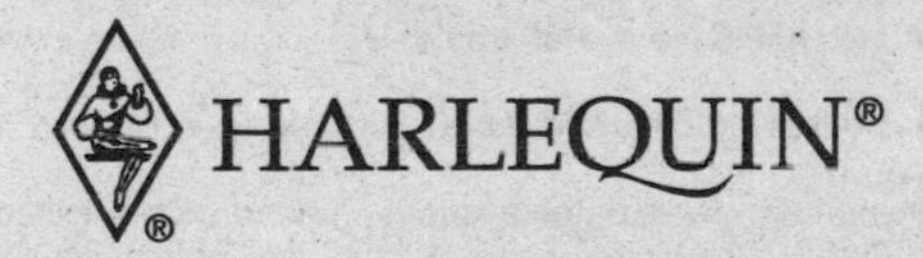

TORONTO • NEW YORK • LONDON
AMSTERDAM • PARIS • SYDNEY • HAMBURG
STOCKHOLM • ATHENS • TOKYO • MILAN • MADRID
PRAGUE • WARSAW • BUDAPEST • AUCKLAND

To Kelly Moses, who embraced me in my new home and who has great strength and a well of courage.

Thanks to firefighter/paramedic Russ Adams for all his assistance with plot details and insight.

ISBN 0-373-69198-X

SPARKING HIS INTEREST

This edition published by arrangement with Harlequin Books S.A.

www.eHarlequin.com

Printed in U.S.A.

1

POLICE LIEUTENANT Wes Kimball slid his truck to a stop behind two patrol cars—the entire force in Baxter, Georgia. The fire department's ladder truck, pump truck and an ambulance completed the collection of city vehicles.

Less than a hundred yards away the warehouse still billowed smoke. By the light of the three-quarter moon, he could see emergency crews lined along the sidewalk—shadows in the night, fighting a battle the heat and flames had already claimed. Still, two teams of firefighters held hoses of streaming water, aiming the quenching drink toward the building's crumbling shell.

Wishing he had a hot cup of coffee, Wes climbed from the truck, then strode purposefully toward the scene. The distinctive smell of gasoline washed over him.

He paused, inhaling deep. Great.

The second fire in as many weeks involving gasoline and a building owned by a prominent Baxter businessman. The second time he'd been called out in the middle of the night to investigate. Last time it was a real estate management office; this time an office supply warehouse. Since he was the only cop in town who worked the arson cases with the fire department, and he'd been dealing with the first fire for the past several days, Wes figured he'd hear from the mayor by dawn. That gave him only three hours to come up with a lead. On four hours sleep.

He hunched his shoulders against the brisk October wind and approached the semicircle of cops standing to the side of the ladder truck. Great beginning for a Tuesday.

"Early enough for you?" Eric Norcutt, a high school buddy and fellow cop, asked.

"Too damn," Wes returned.

Two other members of the Baxter PD snapped to attention.

Wes nodded. "Mornin'."

They returned his nod, saying nothing. Since he was known almost as widely for his formidable temper as his high rate of solved cases, he could hardly object. One of those things he vowed to work on—usually after he'd had a run-in with his boss or his older brother, who was the fire chief.

"What's the word on the warehouse?" Wes asked.

"Dead loss," Norcutt said. "Just like the other place."

A shout rose in the air, then a loud crash. A large beam fell from an upper floor and crumbled to the ground. Still, the firefighters stood their ground, aiming water toward the smoldering building, the picture of proud dedication. No doubt disciples of his brother Ben, who was the spitting image of their heroic father, both of whom Wes had long since ceased trying to live up to. He'd always felt like something of an outsider in his family, probably always would.

Scanning the area again, he stiffened, recognizing two figures standing off to the side. The mayor—whose portly figure was unmistakable—and Robert Addison, the owner of the building, looked to be in deep and intense conversation.

"BFD got here forty minutes ago," Norcutt continued. "They found the warehouse already fully engulfed in flames. Thanks to the drought we had all summer, they're concerned about sparks spreading across the field. They've soaked everything pretty good, but it only takes one."

"And their suspicions?" Wes didn't have to say more than that. Every citizen—law enforcement, fire department or not—knew the first fire had just been declared an arson by the county fire marshal. With the last crime in Baxter involving a farmer's cow being tormented by firecrackers and a couple of intoxicated, idiotic teens, the fire had been the talk of the town.

"*She's* here." Norcutt nodded toward the warehouse. "What's that tell you?"

Wes rolled his shoulders against a twinge of resentment. Well, it seemed his involvement in this case was coming to an end this morning. Didn't matter. He had other cases to deal with. That cow thing for one.

She was Fire Captain Cara Hughes. Presumably, the state's top arson investigator, though he'd personally never worked with her. Ben had consulted her by phone after the last fire and had obviously called her to officially lead the investigation. Wes knew little about her. She was tough—there was even a wild rumor she slept with a six-inch switchblade beneath her pillow—serious and by-the-book.

And she had a rough road ahead. The all-male fire and police force in Baxter would no doubt come up with a few asinine, I-have-two-X-chromosomes-hear-me-roar comments about Hughes's consultation. Personally, Wes didn't care if the arson investigator was an alien with green antennae on his/her/its head.

"Ben called her," Wes said simply.

Norcutt crossed his arms over his beefy chest. "We can handle this."

Technically, an arson case fell under the fire department's jurisdiction. "Probably."

"Ah, hell, Wes, we don't need some woman handling our cases."

"We don't likely have a choice." He cast his gaze toward his friend. "I hear she's really good."

Norcutt rolled his eyes as if saying, how could a *woman* be good at investigating?

"Chill out, Norcutt. I doubt she'll force you to carry her purse."

Norcutt's face turned red. The other guys chuckled.

Deciding he'd had enough male bonding, Wes wandered closer to the warehouse, taking care to stay clear of the firefighters. The smell of smoke, charred wood and gasoline permeated the air. Gas had been the accelerant used in the other fire, though the authorities hadn't suspected arson immediately. People did amazingly stupid things with flammable liquids—storing them next to heaters, by computers, or other types of spark-inducing equipment.

But the first fire had turned out to be no careless accident, and this one smelled like arson, as well.

He'd just rounded the back corner of the warehouse, intent on checking out the receiving docks, when he saw her.

Wearing worn blue jeans, black boots and a black leather jacket, she knelt on the ground in a circular pool of floodlight, which must have been sustained by an alternate power source, since electricity to the building had been long since cut. She had straight, shoulder-length, dark hair, a trim figure and a surprisingly delicate jawline.

She extended her hand, scraping her fingers across the ash-strewn ground, and he noticed a shoulder holster strapped along her left side. Curious. He didn't know any fire people who actually carried a firearm. And no sissy revolver for the lady investigator. From the blue steel butt of the gun, it appeared to be a semiauto pistol.

She glanced up suddenly, her steady gaze locking with his. She was attractive, but not beautiful, yet he found himself unable to look away, as if she held him spellbound with her striking blue-green eyes.

Like the Caribbean sea, he found himself thinking romantically, ridiculously.

"You must be Wes," she said in a husky, sensual voice every bit as gut-clenching as those eyes.

"Yes." He finally found enough of himself to extend his hand. "Wes Kimball."

She rose, shaking his hand briefly. Her skin was smooth and warm, and he was almost disappointed when she dropped her hand by her side. "Cara Hughes. Your brother asked me to take over this case."

Wes slid his hands in the back pockets of his jeans. "I figured as much when I heard you were here."

Her gaze slid to a point over his shoulder, then back to his face. "You've got some kind of welcoming committee."

"This was our case before you got here."

A hint of resentment flashed through those amazing eyes. "This was and still is the fire department's case."

Tough, serious and by-the-book. It was always a shock when the town gossips were actually correct. And, surprisingly, they'd left out all the good stuff—intelligent, obviously dedicated to her job, sensual, slender but curvy. He inclined his head in agreement. "We're just used to handling things ourselves."

"And you don't need some hotshot from Atlanta meddling in your domain?"

He smiled. "I can handle my domain just fine, thank you. You can't tell me you're not used to some resistance."

She crossed her arms over her chest. "Most people stay out of my way actually."

"I guess so, packin' heat at a fire scene."

Her hand slid to her weapon with a casualness that spoke of frequency. Her face flushed. "I forgot it was there. Habit, I guess, going out late at night."

"Important in Atlanta, I'm sure. It sticks out a bit in Baxter." And it turned him on, as if that wasn't weird. He was a cop, could shoot when necessary, but he wasn't any kind of gun buff. He didn't have a collection; he wasn't into hunting. So why did the idea of a woman who treated a pistol with the same familiarity as most women would a watch have desire punch its way into his stomach?

Back to the case, man. You've got no time or call for romance now.

"I guess I don't have to tell you that you're not going to have an easy time of it. This was our case."

She sighed. "This is my case now. And it was and continues to be a fire department case. The police have no—"

"When I said *our*, I meant this town. We've handled arson cases before." Though none with this significance or magnitude.

"You personally?"

"Yes."

"And you don't like giving away your power to an outsider?" She paused. "A woman?"

"I've worked with women before."

She smirked. "When absolutely forced to."

Of course, she assumed the worst about him. And why not? Everybody else did.

He'd admit that at times the strength of his convictions had forced him to rash action or harsh opinions, but he wished he could tap into the part of himself that always made him feel as if he was standing on the other side of the fence from everyone else—especially from his family. He supposed his sometimes defensive position stemmed from losing his father so young in life, from always wanting to live up to his ideal and somehow never seeming to measure up. "Look, I—"

How did he explain solving cases was the only thing that made him feel significant anymore? How to explain what it was like to live in his overachieving family? A brother who was the revered fire chief, a brother-in-law who commanded respect without saying a word, a sister who was a successful businesswoman, another brother who was a firefighter and…well, who commanded respect from every *female* in town.

Simple. He didn't.

She saved him from a graceless reply. "Ben has the right to bring in outside experts if he chooses."

"And you get one more notch on your belt loop?"

If he expected her to flush over his crude analogy, he was dead wrong.

She smiled wide. "You bet your ass."

He found himself returning her smile. And found himself captivated by the humor in her eyes, the curve of her hips, accentuated by her snug jeans. She was really quite…something.

He stepped closer, his heart rate quickening. Her lips parted as she stared up at him, a puff of cloudy-from-the-cold air escaping her mouth. As the scent of gardenias washed over him—an oddly ultrafeminine fragrance coming from such a kick-ass kind of woman—he flexed his fingers, his hands wanting to touch her more than his brain knew was wise. He and Cara seemed suspended like that for several seconds, surrounded by darkness, standing in a puddle of light, smelling the gas and smoke.

It was the smell of petrol that finally brought him to his senses. He stepped back, shoving his hands in his pockets. "So, another arson?"

She blinked, then cleared her throat, as if she'd been caught in the same odd spell as he. "There's enough gasoline to open an Exxon, so it would seem so. I won't know anything for sure until I'm able to get inside the building."

"The sprinkler system was dismantled in the previous fire. The water control valve turned off."

"But not the phone lines to the security system. So when the smoke detectors went off, the system summoned the fire department. Kinda inefficient for an arsonist."

"I guess he didn't realize he had to cut the phone lines, too."

"He knew to cut the chain attached to the water control valve but not the phone or the smoke detectors?" she asked, eyebrows raised.

That point had bothered him after the last fire, as well. "The building's out here in the woods. If the flames burned out of control, it might set off a forest fire."

"So we have an environmentally conscious arsonist?"

"Or someone whose grudge is simply with the owner."

"Robert Addison. What's he like?"

He'd just seen the man practically cheek-to-cheek with the mayor. Hadn't she? "You haven't met him?"

"No."

You haven't missed much. He's a phony jerk, Wes thought, though he controlled the impulse to say so.

"You're obviously not a fan of his."

Surprised, he glanced at her.

"For a cop, your eyes are easy to read."

He was staring into the expressive eyes in this pairing. "And I always thought poker was my game."

She continued to stare at him. Something like interest, raw and sexual, passed through her eyes. "Maybe I'm just more observant than most."

As desire clenched his stomach, his sense of duty to his job and his own needs warred. Though he broke rules more often than he played by them, he wouldn't give in to this attraction. Cara Hughes didn't seem the type to fall for compliments and a nice dinner out. She seemed standoffish and alone. Serious and easy to anger.

Like him.

He was dangerously fascinated by her. This woman with a sharp wit, who carried a pistol and investigated the grim crime of arson.

And did she really feel a connection with him, or was he just impressing his own desires onto her? He was probably making an idiot out of himself, smiling at her, staring at her, his hands itching with the need to touch her. It also occurred to him that he was sharing his theories with someone who could form her own ideas and probably didn't need his two cents.

"Well, I'll let you get to work. I guess I can go back to bed." Wes turned away, an odd sense of loss churning in his belly. He liked her, he realized, and wouldn't have minded working with her. Provided he could set aside the urge to jump her body, of course.

"I could use your help, actually." She said the words quietly, after he'd already walked away a few steps. When he turned back, she continued, "Ben said he'd like for me to have a liaison with the local police."

"Oh, he'll be thrilled you've chosen me."

She angled her head. "He *suggested* you."

Ben? he wanted to repeat incredulously. For total opposites he supposed they got along okay. They'd even come through a weird instance last spring when Ben had married a woman Wes had dated briefly. Unfortunately, they continued to butt heads over everything else. Some part of him recognized they were just different people. They had different outlooks and temperaments. Ben valued conservatism and professionalism, and Wes tended to be more progressive and less likely to follow the rules. He really wanted just to sit down over a cold Budweiser and tell his brother all the insecurities and live-up-to-the-Kimball-heroism anxieties he had, but he hadn't.

Probably because the conflict had run for many years, back to when Ben had been forced to take over as the leader of their family, when their father had died fighting a fire and their mother had fallen apart and retreated emotionally from all of them.

Wes's resentment over being bossed by his brother no doubt stemmed from their differing personalities as well as the closeness in their ages. Their younger brother, Steve, who was also a firefighter, never seemed to have conflicts with anyone. Everybody loved him. Everybody wanted to be around him. Why couldn't he follow Steve's example?

Cara stepped toward him, reminding him he had other issues on his plate. "Robert Addison."

Wes bobbed his head back. "He's standing over there. Ask him yourself."

Her gaze shifted. "He's here?"

"Talking to the mayor. It's Addison's building. Somebody called him, I guess."

"I guess," she said, then shook her head. "I'll get to him. Right now, I want to know what *you* think."

Figuring he would regret his honesty, he plunged

forward anyway. "He wears expensive clothes, drives a flashy car, owns a huge plantation house on a big hill. I'll bet his underwear has designer logos on them. He's sophisticated and smooth." He paused, his gaze shifting to her face. "The ladies seem to like him."

She rolled her eyes. "Yippee. Just how wealthy are we talking about here?"

Addison wouldn't be the first to target his own property for gain, he supposed. "Several million."

"Business stable?"

"He's well diversified."

"Bad habits?"

He really liked her suspicious nature. "Not that I know of."

"Nothing you can prove, you mean."

Nothing he could even substantiate. Other than one personal experience, it was just a feeling. A gut reaction that said *slime* whenever Addison was around. Expensive slime, but still messy. Wes just plain didn't like the guy as a person, as a man, so that opinion clouded any judgment of him the cop could form.

She paced next to him, her boots crunching against the gravel mixed with grass. "What about enemies?"

"Those he's got plenty of."

She stopped. Her eyes gleamed—like a hunter's. "Yeah?"

"He's rich, so some people automatically resent that. He's fired people over the years. More resentment. He treats people as if they're beneath him. And I—" He stopped. That was private. And old news.

"What? Why do I get the feeling there's something personal here?"

He should have known she wouldn't let that slide. "I just don't like him."

"He doesn't sound like a likeable guy."

You let your feelings get messed up with your professional judgment. The sheriff, his brother, even the mayor had said those words so often to him, he'd lost count. Did people really do that—separate the personal from the professional? Did other cops really look at rapists and think, *He's broken the law, violated a woman's body, her personal safety* and not think, *He's a scumbag who ought to be locked up for life?*

I don't think so.

To hell with it. "He's not a likeable guy," Wes said, meeting her gaze.

"And there are plenty of other people who feel that way."

"I don't doubt it."

"Hmm." She smiled suddenly, and he found the expression all the more welcoming considering their surroundings. All the more alluring because of the sober expression he'd first encountered. "At least we won't have a lack of suspects."

He returned her smile. "Probably not."

She drew a breath, and again her eyes reflected more than just an interest in the case. He hadn't imagined the glimpse of desire this time. The big question was: what were they going to do about it?

"It's going to be interesting working with you, Lieutenant."

He took a step closer to her. "You, too."

His heart thudded as his gaze roved her face. He was crazy, feeling like this. So quickly. So intensely. He'd never worked with anyone he was attracted to.

Could he ignore the sparks of attraction? Be professional? Reserved? He very nearly winced.

He'd have to. This case was the most intriguing to come along in a long time. And if he managed to slide in a dig or two, a moment of trouble for Robert Addison…all the better.

Her gaze slid to a point over his shoulder. Her eyes narrowed. She laid her hands on her hips and squinted. "Is there a reason Elvis would have an interest in this fire?"

Wes didn't bother to turn around. Yep, life was about to get really interesting. "Oh, yeah. He's the mayor."

"WES, I'M SURE you'll be fully prepared to explain this latest assault on our formerly secure community by 9:00 a.m. in my office," the man, presumably the mayor, announced as he swaggered toward them. "Mr. Addison is very disturbed by this latest attack."

Cara stared at him. She'd seen a lot of wild—and gruesome—things in her career, but a portly mayor in a white polyester beaded jumpsuit, slick, black-dyed hair, with long sideburns and big gold sunglasses at an arson scene at two-thirty in the morning was a new one.

"Of course, Mayor Collins." Wes gestured to her. "Have you met Cara Hughes? She's the state's foremost arson investigator. She'll be taking over the case."

Cara shot Wes a look of retribution. *Turn me over to the nutty mayor, will you? I'll remember that.*

The mayor settled his hands on his hips, which pushed back the white cape attached to the jumpsuit, and highlighted the large, rhinestone-studded belt buckle imprinted with the letters *TCB,* which stood for Taking Care of Business, if her Elvis lore was on track. Even through the sunglasses, Cara could sense his measuring gaze. She waited in silence imagining what he was thinking while he looked his fill. *Who are you? What would drive a woman to do this? Why aren't you home raising babies or teaching school like a decent, small-town Southern woman?* Many a foster parent and supervisor had questioned her idiosyncrasies over the years. She was long immune, and it was always interesting to see where each person categorized her.

Elvis the Mayor chose to ignore her.

"Baxter is a safe town," he said to Wes. "I don't need this in the papers in the morning."

"It's still safe," Wes said, his deep blue eyes full of a violent restraint that was no doubt lost on the mayor.

Cara, however, found his emotional state fascinating.

She could all but reach out and touch the suppressed need for respect, success and, ultimately, acceptance on his face. Since she understood those emotions probably better than anyone, they were easy to spot in other people. Wes wouldn't likely be thrilled that she suspected his secret, but then she never intended to get close enough to tell him. And maybe she'd just read too much into the moment.

"I see we've all met," Ben said as he approached them in a full turn-out of fireproof coat, pants, hat and gloves. He barely glanced at his brother, though he'd bragged earlier about what an excellent liaison he'd make for her. Then again, he didn't pay much attention to the mayor. Of course, that could be because he couldn't keep a straight face and talk to the mayor at the same time.

"Yes, sir," she said, "but I'm anxious to get inside the building."

"Go ahead. Start on the right side of the building, the entrance to the office. It's untouched over there. I've still got men checking the building's stability in the warehouse section. They'll give you clearance when they can."

Cara nodded, pulling the architectural drawings of the building from inside her jacket pocket.

"What are your first impressions?" Ben asked.

"No mistaking the gas. Like last time, I expect." She glanced briefly at the mayor. She didn't make snap judgments about fire scenes or—usually—people, but she wasn't sure how in the loop Elvis was. "I'll know more in a day or so."

Ben nodded and smiled slightly, his teeth glowing white behind his soot-stained face. "Fine." He paused, turning to Elvis. "Mayor Collins, I know you're anxious to let these two get to work."

He nodded at Cara and Wes. "Of course. Mr. Addison and I both expect solid leads right away."

"I understand Mr. Addison is here at the scene?" Cara asked.

"He was, but he left. He's a busy man, you know."

What pressing business he could possibly have at this hour of the morning, Cara couldn't imagine. He had to have realized the investigators would want to talk to him, leaving her to wonder why he'd avoided them.

The mayor turned away with Ben, muttering

about the wisdom of outsiders and rebels in the middle of the most important investigation of the year.

"You must be the outsider," Wes said.

"Ah, then you're the rebel," Cara returned in mock surprise. "I'd wondered."

Wes extended his hand toward the building. "Shall we?"

She regarded him closely, the loose gray sweatshirt and jean jacket covering his chest, the worn jeans caressing his legs, the wildness in his eyes, the dark shadow of a closely cropped goatee surrounding his sensual mouth, the windblown hair. He added up to trouble with a capital *T*. She rarely noticed the men she worked with. Why him? Why now?

She shook aside the desire fluttering in her belly. Her single-minded focus on her job would obviously serve her well during this investigation. "Lead on."

They walked maybe fifty feet to the still-smoldering building, Cara consulting her diagram along the way.

"The manager's office is through here," she said as they approached the door, which was fully intact and propped open by a rock. "Not much of an office. The building's mostly warehouse space."

Wes held open the door. "After you, Captain."

Over her shoulder, Cara glanced at him, noticing the amused but exasperated look on his face. "Damn titles," she muttered. "Makes me feel like saluting."

He smiled widely, and she felt a sudden kinship with him, as if he, too, thought all the posturing of most people in public service was ridiculous. "Hmm. Ms. Hughes, then?" He paused. "Or maybe...*Cara*."

Hearing her name fall so easily and seductively from his lips gave her a jolt she hadn't expected. Her name had never sounded exotic. Intimate. Warmth spread through her body before she could stop it.

Still, she narrowed her eyes as she said, "Too bad we have to stick with the titles to maintain professional integrity." She returned her attention to the diagram, determined not to let him know he'd rattled her.

"And the saluting?"

She glanced back up. He was still smiling—just barely, but seductively, invitingly.

She couldn't imagine Wes Kimball saluting for anyone, so the question seemed irrelevant. And just why was the lieutenant flirting with her?

Usually she expended little effort holding people at a distance. Yet somehow, he'd managed to step into her personal space with a couple of words and without moving physically closer.

"No sal—" She stopped as she crossed the office's threshold. Water squished through the carpet beneath her boots. Small puddles covered the beige steel desk sitting just inside the door. The ink on the desk calendar had smeared to nearly unrecognizable scrawls. Water still dripped from the sprinkler heads mounted to the ceiling.

"He's not a very thorough arsonist, is he?" Wes said dryly from behind her.

Picturing the damage to the outside of the building, the half-dozen firefighters still battling the aftereffects of the blaze, the stress and suspicion that was likely to overwhelm the mayor, the town and the investigators, Cara sighed. "Looks like he's two for two to me."

CARA'S GAZE slid
damage and the c
damage. Her mind ... ities
of a destroyed ware... emergency
alert system and work ...rs—at least in this
part of the building.

"There's more than one control valve," she said slowly, glancing down at the architectural plans in her hands for confirmation.

Wes wandered around the soaked room, shaking his head. "So he dismantled the sprinklers in the warehouse, turning off the water valve in there, but left the phone lines intact and this valve on?"

"Makes sense to me. Maybe he didn't know about this one."

"Maybe," he said, though he didn't sound convinced.

Maybe was fine with Cara for now. Questions without answers were fine. She'd interpret once she had more facts.

"Check to see if the door leading to the warehouse is locked," she said as she headed toward the supply closet door near the back left corner of the room. "Be careful not to smudge any prints," she added, tosses from her jacket

ore," he said, sounding an-

an you've done it right."

n do it right."

paused in the process of slipping on her own ir of gloves. The man had totally messed with her mind, since his innocent words had sparked a carnal angle. She *had* to get him back into his spot as professional assistant—fast. "Just check the locks, Lieutenant."

She flung open the closet door, noting the supply closet was big—about twelve by twelve—nearly the same size as the office. It was full of file cabinets mostly. But against one wall sat a bright, orange-red, floor-to-ceiling pipe that was connected to the wall via a few small pipes.

Heart pounding, she strode towards the pipe, her gaze zeroing in on the pressure gauge window, then to the chain fastened to the water control valve knob, which was about the size of a car steering wheel. The chain held the knob in place, so the water pressure couldn't be turned off accidentally. Cutting it, unfortunately, was easy—a pair of wire clippers would do. Newer systems had an antitamper device so that if the chain was cut an alarm went off. Until she examined the main security panel she wouldn't know if that was the case here.

"Found it, huh?" Wes said from behind her. "Works, I guess."

"There's plenty of water pressure. The chain's intact. What about the door?"

"Unlocked, but shut. Why?"

Still studying the pipe system for anything unusual, she replied, "I'm not worried about why yet. I'm still absorbing."

"Absorbing?"

She drew in a quick breath, and her thought process shut down. She hadn't realized he was so close. She even thought she could feel his breath against the back of her neck. Impossible. Her hair and the collar of her jacket kept any skin from exposure. She was imagining things. Dreaming.

"Not that I'm an expert or anything—my last fire investigation involved some dingbat woman who set fire to her house to get the insurance money...."

At his tone, Cara turned her head to look at him. Big mistake. He rolled his pretty blue eyes—a description he would no doubt hate—and shoved his hands into the back pockets of his jeans, drawing her gaze to the breadth of his shoulders, which tapered to a lean waist—

She forced her gaze immediately back to his face. She wasn't some chick on the make, drawn to the moodiness and danger that rolled off Wes Kimball in waves. The aura of confidence and vulnerability—

She stopped her thoughts again. What the hell was wrong with her?

"...caught on to her scheme after about two and a half minutes," Wes continued, seeming not to notice her straying concentration. "But doesn't all this seem like overkill?" He frowned. "Or just confusing? If I'm setting a fire in a warehouse, I toss out the gasoline, cut the chain, turn off the water. No water, no sprinklers. The fire will spread rapidly. Then I go to the system panel, bust it open, pull out every wire I can get my hands on and hightail it out of there. Fire rages. Property's a dead loss. No fire department to get in the way."

Cara had several problems with that theory, but she jumped on to the most obvious one first. She really liked running through the possible scenarios with him. Usually, she had to play devil's advocate with herself. "And how would you know to cut the chain to the water valve?"

"The Internet. There's probably a damn Web site—www dot set-a-fire dot com."

"And that step-by-step instruction would leave out the smoke detector, the fire department alert system—which is useless without telephone wires—and the possibility of a second control valve? And then, of course, we have the motive to consider. Was the fire department's arrival a mistake? *Twice?* Why this warehouse, why the office last week—"

Wes raised his hand to stop her questions, then rubbed his temples. "There are dozens of angles, aren't there?"

"Even angles that don't involve Addison's guilt?"

He said nothing for a moment, then shook his head. "I don't see any."

She was dying to ask him what had made him so biased against Addison, what past they had forged, but, following her own advice, she kept her suspicions at bay. They were gathering evidence. Interpretation came later.

"So what do we know?" she asked. "For instance, the day-to-day operations."

"It's an office supply warehouse. Lots of crates

and boxes moving around. Trucks arriving to deliver inventory ordered from manufacturers. Trucks arriving to pick up and distribute supplies to various businesses in town and out."

"Exactly." She paced along the far wall, more in an attempt to escape the enticing scent of his cologne, or soap, or something than the need to move. "Kind of a humdrum existence. Items come in, items move out. Then inventory a few times a year. So who are the people who do all this moving about?"

"Some warehouse people, a manager…"

Cara tucked her map away and pulled her PDA from her jacket pocket, handing it to Wes, knowing the info regarding this particular property of Robert Addison's was displayed on the screen.

Wes stared at the screen. "This is the background check I ran after the first fire."

"Ben e-mailed it to me." She continued pacing. "So, employees consist of the manager, his assistant and five warehouse personnel. All work a day shift. After five o'clock, the property is deserted. The only other people with access to the building are the cleaning service, which comes once a week. The property is protected by a decent security system, which is connected to the fire alert system."

"Captain Hughes?" someone called from the other room.

Cara strode from the closet and saw a firefighter, who was unmistakably a Kimball, peeking around the door between the office and the warehouse. "Yes?"

The man nodded. "It's safe for you to come out here now, though I wouldn't delay too long. The steel reinforcements are holding things up for the moment. They seem solid, but with the heat of the fire..." He shrugged his broad shoulders.

"Thanks. I'll hurry," she said.

"We'll be around a while still. Holler if you need us." Then he grinned, his Kimball blue eyes twinkling. "And Wes says he gets all the lousy assignments."

He strode off, and Cara turned, nearly bumping into Wes. The man was forever sneaking up on her. She extended her hands to keep her balance, encountered Wes's chest, then pulled back just as quickly and swayed on her feet.

He grabbed her shoulders. "That's my younger brother, Steve."

Still a little dizzy by the idea of nearly being held in his arms, Cara simply nodded. "I figured. Monica said there were three of you."

His hands, still resting on her shoulders, tensed. "I didn't realize you knew my sister-in-law."

"We met a few months ago when she redecorated several firehouses in Atlanta." She stared up at him. She knew Monica had briefly dated Wes, though everyone seemed to agree the match had been a mistake. "Problem?"

"No. I just can't picture the two of you as friends."

"We're certainly different." But outrageous Monica made her smile, and her new friend was always talking about shoes or wallpaper—a nice change from gasoline and matches. She wondered, however, if the tension she'd sensed between Wes and Ben had something to do with Monica. "I understand she and Ben eloped in Vegas."

"They were all googly-eyed about it. Weird."

Okay. Strike one with that theory. Wes obviously

wasn't pining after his sister-in-law. The brothers probably just had a personality conflict. Wes seemed to share little with Mr. Professionally Reserved Fire Chief Ben.

When she turned, Wes had to drop his hold on her. She didn't like being that close to him, touching him. She had a job to do, which didn't involve examining the personal lives of her colleagues. She'd taken several steps toward the door to the warehouse when he asked, "How, exactly, does a sprinkler system work?"

She glanced back, noting he stood by a large, black file cabinet on the other side of the manager's desk. "When it detects fire, it shoots water everywhere."

"Not exactly. It detects *heat*. And it's the water flow that actually triggers the alarm." Confidence suffused his face as he met her gaze. "Right?"

"Right."

"And here we have water flow, so the fire department came, just like the first fire."

"Right again." She paused. "He obviously didn't know about the possibility of a second water valve."

"I don't think so." He pointed at the ground, and she walked around the edge of the desk to see what was so interesting.

A metal trash can was filled with ashes and sitting on the floor beside the file cabinet. "What the hell..."

"Look up."

She tipped back her head, focusing on the sprinkler head just above them. "He set the sprinklers off on purpose." Her gaze met his. "He *wanted* the fire department to come."

"Interesting, don't you think?"

"Oh, yeah." She paused, trying to minimize the

sweet thrill of discovery coursing through her veins. They still had a lot of investigating to do, but she definitely had a feel for this arsonist. What he wanted, what turned him on. It was this part of the job that she liked, the part that made her so successful. She headed toward the door leading to the warehouse. "Let's see what else we find."

She snagged two hard hats from a rack on the wall, handing one to Wes. "You know the drill, I'm sure. Safety first. Keep your eyes and ears open for any shifting debris."

A half smile hovered on the lieutenant's lips. "It's not so bad working with you, actually."

"So glad you think so. I'll be sure to pass that along to my CO."

"Who *is* your CO?" he asked as she gingerly turned the doorknob.

"Technically, the state fire marshal, but the governor's put me in charge of several task forces lately."

"*The* governor? Of the state?"

She laid one hand on her hip. "He *likes* working with me."

His gaze raked her figure, somehow communicating admiration without insolence. "I imagine he does."

Her face heated. She was blushing? Oh, man, that was too much. "Come on, hotshot, let's find the security panel."

Thankfully, he fell into step beside her and didn't comment on the personal turn the conversation had taken. "Any idea where to look?"

Cara glanced at the ruined space surrounding her,

then consulted her map again. "Looks like we have a sprinkler room toward the back, closer to the left side."

They headed in that direction, picking their way around the boxes reduced to near ashes. With smoke still lingering in the air, water dripping off most everything, the ceiling partially collapsed in some places, they had a hard time figuring out what was what.

After several minutes of winding through collapsed and melting rows of giant metal storage shelves without any luck, Wes said, "I'll find Steve. Maybe he knows where the room is."

"Good idea. I'll keep looking."

She headed off again, stepping over boxes and piles of still-smoldering paper, wondering just how many tons of supplies had fallen from upper floors and how much had actually been down here to start with. It was all a blackened, ashy, damp mess.

But just as she was about to turn a corner partially blocked by a fallen beam, she saw a glint of gold. A doorknob maybe?

She squinted, picking up a crumpled box and moving it aside. The outline of a door was definitely visible just behind a group of boxes. Moving them aside one by one, she finally made a small path for her to squeeze through.

Sweat rolled down her face as she struggled toward her goal. She bent over a bit, dusting the soot from her jeans. As she straightened, she saw the body.

The slumped, badly burned figure against the wall. It was a man. It used to be a man.

She turned her head, swallowing the urge to gag. She'd seen it before, would no doubt see it again. The man wasn't there anymore. Just his body, the flesh that used to contain him. Still, she had to draw a few deep breaths through her mouth before she knew she could look back.

Her gaze slid back to his face, charred and ruined.

Was this how the investigator had felt when he'd found her parents? Revolted, yet full of pity, praying they hadn't suffered?

"Lieutenant!" she called, then let her head fall back as she stared at the blackened ceiling, trying to calm her breathing.

"Not far behind you," he called. "You're nearly on top of the security system room."

She knew the moment he'd made it past the boxes. He sucked a breath; the air stilled.

"This thing just got a whole lot more serious," he said.

She glanced at him over her shoulder. "It certainly did."

WES STARED OUT his truck's windshield as he drove himself and Cara through the predawn light.

They'd said very little to each other in the past three hours. Words were certainly beyond him, though he did wonder how often she found something as horrible as what they'd just witnessed. His thoughts went to his father, of course, tragically killed in a fire when Wes was just a teenager. He thanked God he'd never seen him like that.

As he turned off the deserted highway and headed into town, he also realized he could be thankful he hadn't disgraced himself or embarrassed Cara. Seeing the shock and horror on her face, he'd swallowed hard. He'd let the part of him that had always been a cop take over. He hadn't drawn her into his arms the way he'd wanted. He'd relied on stark professionalism as they examined the body for evidence and identification and waited for the coroner and ambulance.

Unable to find ID, Cara had ordered the victim be sent directly to the hospital morgue for autopsy. Poor old Doc Moses, who served as the town's coroner, had never seen anything like this horribly disfigured body. He'd mumbled and stumbled, and Cara had pulled him aside while the paramedics bagged the body for transport.

Then, patting Doc's hand, she'd told him to go on home. She'd call one of the state's forensic experts to do the autopsy and have him rush to Baxter immediately.

She'd been brave and lovely, and Wes found himself falling even more thoroughly under her spell.

"After you drop me off at the hospital, go home and get some rest," she said quietly. "I'll call you when I have news."

"I'm going to the firehouse." At least they'd have food and company. "Why don't you come with me? You can shower, get some coffee..."

But she was already shaking her head. "I told the pathologist I'd meet him at the hospital. Hopefully, he'll have preliminary results sometime tomorrow."

He simply nodded.

"You mind if I roll down the window a bit?" she asked, not looking at him.

"Go ahead." With the scent of smoke still permeating his clothes, some fresh air would no doubt do them both good. The crisp air hit him, shocking his thoughts and senses into clarity. Her hair billowed away from her face, highlighting her pale skin and watery eyes. Again, the need to touch her washed over him.

He gripped the steering wheel tighter. She was a colleague, not a date. "You want some company at the hospital?"

"No, thanks. I need to be alone. I need to think."

Wes didn't argue, though he wanted to leave her about as much as he wanted to find another body in the warehouse rubble.

So it must have been self-preservation that made him press harder on the gas.

HOURS LATER, Wes found himself staring out another window. This time it was Ben's office window at the firehouse. The sky blazed a brilliant October blue. Not a cloud floated on the horizon. The sun was bright, almost stark white, so powerful he had to squint to look at it.

If he stared intensely enough would he forget the sight of the body? He hoped so, since every time he closed his eyes that's all he saw.

As a result, he'd never gone back to sleep. It was three o'clock in the afternoon, and he still had no desire to lie down, even though Ben had tried to push him to get some rest. The only concession he'd made was to shower and borrow some clean clothes.

Cara had just called Ben from the hospital. She had some preliminary results, and she was on her way to see them.

In the hours they'd been apart, Wes had managed to rebottle his emotions. They'd been through a charged and shocking situation together; it was only natural he'd felt a certain kinship with her. Their thought processes and dispositions were similar so, of course, he'd been drawn to her. They were virtually in the same business so, of course, they understood each other. But in a normal situation, if he'd spotted her at the grocery store or in a bar, he wouldn't have done more than smile politely. This clawing, aching need to see her again, to finally, fully touch her skin was nothing more than a human reaction to a stressful situation.

He'd had more bad endings to relationships in the past year than he'd had in his whole life. Some bad *and* embarrassing endings. Monica came to mind. It was enough to put a man off women. Well, almost.

And he remembered Cara knew her. Monica and Cara. He found that combination hard to mesh. On the other hand, outrageous Monica had married conservative Ben, and they were happy, so what did he know about the subtleties of the heart? He was better off alone. Always had been. Probably always would be.

The office door swung open. Steve stuck his head inside. "Wanna get a beer later?"

"Yeah. Maybe. If I'm awake later."

"You can tell me all about the sexy Captain Hughes."

"She's here to work, not date the locals." *Oh, Mr. Righteous, are we?* You, *however, can come on to her all you like.* He refused to acknowledge his conscience trying to tell him that he just didn't need Steve's competition. Women fell at the guy's feet on a daily basis. "Watch yourself, baby brother, she's armed."

"Sounds like a challenge."

Whatever additional warning Wes would have

liked to issue was interrupted by the mayor and Ben brushing by Steve as they entered the office.

"Ben," the mayor said as he waddled across the room, "I just don't see how this woman, this *outsider* can do a better job than your folks here."

Steve grinned, then retreated quickly, closing the door.

The mayor went on, "She sent Doc Moses into a near faint with that body business."

Before Wes could defend Cara or explain the situation the mayor had—as usual—gotten wrong, Ben spoke up. "Doc's the coroner. By law we have to call him to the scene. Captain Hughes has graciously offered to assist in the investigation by bringing in one of her colleagues for the autopsy."

"Oh, hello, Wes," the mayor said absently, plopping into a chair in front of Ben's desk. "Glad you're here. I'm sure you'll be on my side in this."

Wes met Ben's gaze over the mayor's head. His brother shook his head.

Striving to take his brother's silent advice, Wes didn't comment, though where the mayor got that Wes of all people would be on his side, he hadn't a clue. At least the mayor's presence had driven all self-pitying, morose thoughts from his mind. No one could keep from smiling in the presence of a man in a lime-green polyester jumpsuit with bright orange rhinestones, turquoise braided trim and pink sunglasses.

"We have a murder to investigate," Wes began. "We're all on the same side."

The mayor sighed into his jowls. "Yes, yes, of course. Any idea who he was?"

"There was no ID on the body," Ben said. "Captain Hughes told me only that he was male, Caucasian, probably between forty-five and fifty. Mr. Addison has been contacted, and he's spoken with his managers. None of the employees are unaccounted for, so we're going to put the dental records into a national database."

The mayor winced. "Dental records. I can't believe this is happening in Baxter."

Ben sank into the chair behind his desk. He, too, hadn't slept. "I know. It's been a rough night for everyone."

"Mr. Addison will demand quick answers," the mayor added.

Wes, who still hadn't moved from his position in front of the window, couldn't resist this time. "He'll have to wait in line."

The mayor glanced up at him, surprise evident in his eyes. "Wes, you know as well as I do how important Mr. Addison is to this community. It's thanks to his civic generosity that we have a new communications system in the police station."

Wes ground his teeth. "I'm well aware of his contribution."

"Tax dollars are simply not enough," the mayor continued, obviously not aware of Wes's gathering temper. "Without cooperation from the business community we can't move our town forward."

Wes was all for moving forward, and he couldn't deny the equipment was cutting-edge, but in his experience, ultragenerous gifts of thousands of dollars never arrived without a cost. Especially from a blowhard like Addison. Wes had been waiting nearly four months to find out just when Addison would ask for his favor. The passing of time had only made him more itchy, wondering just how much the businessman expected in return from the Baxter Police Department.

"Personally," he said, crossing his arms over his chest and leaning against the window, "I think it will be interesting to see just how anxious Addison is to get this case solved."

The mayor sat erect, even as Ben sighed. "What do you mean by that? The last thing I need is my peace officers making attacks against our citizens. We must all put up a brave front in this time of crisis."

Ben held up his hand. "Mayor, let's please not jump to conclusions about anyone or anything." He directed his gaze to Wes, giving him no doubt that he was included in this warning. "We don't need the newspaper to get wind of any more problems. I understand from a friend at the paper that the Atlanta media have been calling them all afternoon for updates. Their cameras are imminent. We all need to be professional and resolute in this."

Wes had been pushed beyond his already shaky patience. He wanted to scream, to explode. He stalked across the room. "*You* be professional. *I'll* be pissed. A man has lost his life. There's an arsonist running loose in our town." He yanked open the door. "We have to—"

He ground to a halt, encountering Cara on the other side of the door. Her hand was raised to knock.

"Oh, hi," she said. Her eyes were droopy and bloodshot, her skin pale.

"You—" He stopped. Her exhaustion was none of his business. She was a trained expert. She didn't need him babying her. "Come on in."

Ben and the mayor both stood up as she walked into the room, with Ben offering her the chair next to the mayor. "Coffee?" he asked.

She shook her head. "I've had too much already."

"What do you know about the victim?" Ben asked.

Wes returned to his place by the window, all thoughts of storming out gone. Ridiculous, this need to be near her. But there it was. Undeniable.

"Not too much," Cara said. "He definitely died of smoke inhalation. He probably never even woke up. He had holes in the bottoms of his shoes and several of his teeth were rotten. I think he was a homeless person or drifter, who wandered in looking for a warm place to sleep. The lock on the back door had been jimmied, so he probably sneaked in that way. The warehouse manager confirmed having to run out a man who fits his general description a couple of weeks ago."

"Any chance he's the arsonist?" the mayor asked, wringing his chubby hands.

"It's possible, I guess, though no traces of gasoline were found on his hands or clothes."

"You don't think he's responsible?" Ben asked.

"No, I don't."

Wes kept silent. He'd have the opportunity to argue his point about Addison being the prime suspect, but he had no intention of doing so in front of the mayor. They'd already had an argument about this after the first fire. Wes had made the mistake of pointing out that Addison had had the property up for sale a few months before and hadn't been successful in dumping it, and wasn't it convenient that the property was now a complete loss?

The resulting diatribe, complete with horror at the quick, wrongful judgment of a generous (aka rich) law-abiding citizen, still rang in his ears.

The mayor bit his lip, then glanced at his watch. "Good grief, I'm going to be late to the garden club luncheon." He shook his head. "And I must say, it's a measure of how upset we all are that no one commented on my garden motif suit." He waddled out.

For the first time since their horrible discovery in the warehouse, Wes met Cara's gaze, and they shared a smile.

"Don't start with me—either one of you," Ben said, obviously noting their amusement. "You haven't had to listen to him moan about the upcoming elections, about how he's dedicated his whole life to this town and how that 'young, whippersnapper lawyer' running against him will use these fires to prove he can't maintain order and safety."

"I've been at the morgue, you know," Cara pointed out.

"And I've been..." Wes began. Actually, he'd been brooding. "I got chewed out after the last fire."

Ben went on as if he hadn't heard them. "And the whole time he's rambling I'm thinking, *Where exactly does he get those suits?* I mean does he have them made? I can't imagine a store carrying them in inventory."

Wes crossed the room, sitting on the edge of Ben's desk. He hadn't seen his brother this messed up since the day he'd asked for advice about dating Monica. "Cheer up, Chief. It could be worse."

"I don't see how."

Wes fought back laughter. "The whippersnapper lawyer could be a big Kiss fan."

Ben groaned, then narrowed his eyes at Cara. "You look terrible."

She blinked, then glared back. "Gee, thanks."

Ben's face flushed. "Sorry. You just—" He stopped, looking to Wes for support.

Wes simply shook his head.

"You need some rest," Ben said, gazing unflinchingly at Cara.

Brave guy, Wes thought. *That pistol is within easy reach.*

Ben began writing on a slip of paper. "These are directions to my house. I want you to go back to the apartment you're renting, sleep for at least four hours, then come to my house for dinner at seven." He extended the paper, which Cara took. "That's an order."

Cara clamped her jaw tight, but managed to ask, "Is there a room I could use here? I'd rather be close if a lead develops. And I'm fine with ordering pizza and meeting in your office."

"I'm fine with pizza, too, but my wife has other ideas, as I'm sure you can imagine."

Cara nodded. "I'll be there."

"Wes, can you come to dinner, too? We'll have some privacy to discuss the case at length."

Wes noticed his brother asked him rather than demanded, even though the jurisdiction of the case allowed him to command the police however he saw fit. It was this unfailingly polite, restrained tone that set Wes's teeth on edge. Their teasing over the mayor seemed forgotten, replaced by the usual tension.

He shoved aside the trouble. "I'll find you a room," he said to Cara.

She rose. "Chief" was all she said to Ben in parting. She didn't speak to Wes either until he stopped outside a private room decorated in blue and gray and resembling a small hotel suite, including a computer and entertainment center and a bathroom off to the right. "Nice room. Does everybody else's look like this?" she asked suspiciously, as if wary of special treatment.

"No, the guys sleep in a one-room bunk hall. This would be for our female firefighters—if we had any."

She raised her eyebrows.

Her silence unnerved him. No one could ever accuse him of being the most talkative person in a crowd, so carrying the conversation didn't set well with him.

"They keep bringing the local school kids through here on field trips, thinking someday surely one of the girls will see the job's appeal."

"Hmm," she said as she wandered into the room.

Wes stayed in the doorway. All these weird, gut-clenching feelings kept slamming into him when he looked at her. The lust he understood, could even embrace, if it wasn't for this case they were working together. But he wanted to sit her down and get her life story. He wanted to know what had driven her to become an arson investigator. He wanted to know her favorite foods, movies and books. He wanted to tuck her into bed and watch those shrewd, expressive eyes close in sleep.

Obviously through exploring the room, she faced him. "You've been with me more than Ben. Do I look exhausted?"

"Yes."

"Why didn't *you* tell me to lie down?"

"It would piss me off, so I knew it would piss you off. I'll see you at dinner." He backed out, closing the door as he went, wondering how he could possibly already have such a strong sense of her.

And wondering why he was walking away instead of running.

3

CARA RAISED her hand to ring the doorbell at Ben and Monica's house. Then, just as quickly, dropped her hand by her side.

"This is ridiculous," she muttered.

She was actually nervous about this meeting. *He* was coming. That annoyingly sexy and intriguing Wes Kimball. When she looked at him every professional thought in her head ran like crazy for higher ground.

She did *not* get in a lather about men. The few relationships she'd experienced had been brief, all ending when the man in question couldn't seem to grasp the concept that her career was the highest priority in her life. And she hadn't met one yet to cause her to reconsider the idea.

"You're being an idiot, Cara."

With her index finger, she punched the doorbell a little harder than necessary and wondered if the rosy lipstick she'd added after a quick shower at her apartment was already smudged as usual.

Monica opened the door—thank God. "Cara!" She grabbed her into a quick hug. "Don't you look great. That lipstick is just the perfect shade."

Oh, goody, that mystery was solved. Now she could sleep nights.

But while she rolled her eyes regarding her own spurt of vanity, she reveled in Monica's. Her friend wore a clingy white sweater, a purple leather miniskirt and matching purple stilettos. Her long red hair was curled and sensuously framed her striking face, highlighting her bright green eyes.

How she was going to discuss a fatal arson case with two men in this woman's presence, though, Cara had no idea.

In the foyer, she slid out of her jacket, then handed her friend the bottle of champagne she'd picked up at the liquor store.

If possible, Monica brightened even more. "Oooh! I haven't had champagne in ages. You'll share with me, won't you?"

Cara glanced around the lovely, two-story foyer, her gaze jumping from detail to detail. Lots of wood and windows, great rich colors of dark green, claret and gold. Monica's impeccable taste as a decorator was obvious. "One glass. I've got case files to go through."

Monica stuck out her tongue. "You can't work all night."

"And I've got to drive home."

"Home? To Atlanta? You can't—"

Cara held up her hand. "I rented an apartment in town."

"Oh, good. It'll be nice having you so close."

Her friend's enthusiasm helped Cara to finally set aside the stomach-rolling memories of last night. "So, what's for dinner?"

"Ben and Wes are outside on the deck, grilling something. I'm not really sure what. I tried to tell them that for dinner parties these days people order in, then fix everything on silver platters to make it look like you'd slaved in the kitchen all day. But they pointed out the limited selection of 'ordering in' places in Baxter. I mean this town sells live bait in vending machines. Where are we going to order a respectable dinner?"

"Live bait?"

"Yep. Ben assured me that all real men knew how to grill, so I poured a glass of wine and left them to it."

"Excellent idea," Cara said as they walked into the kitchen.

The room stole her breath. Dark oak cabinets and floors, stone countertops, stainless steel appliances, more warm touches of red and gold, artistic bowls and accessories, and to one side an octagon-shaped cupola with a glass ceiling and glass walls. It looked like one of those kitchens on the Home and Garden channel.

She walked into the cupola, absorbing the clear, twinkling view of the lake on the other side of the windows. She felt as if she were suspended over the lake, nothing but water beneath her and sky above.

"What do you think?" Monica asked from behind her.

Cara spun to face her. "Wow."

Her friend beamed.

The back door swung open, and Ben's voice floated into the room "...a pretty good game, but—" Ben himself appeared, holding a bottle of beer in one hand and a platter of steaks in the other. He smiled at Cara. "Good. You're here. And looking rested."

"Thanks." Though she'd been aggravated as hell that he'd ordered her to take a break, she had to admit he'd been right. The moment she'd woken from her nap, her theory about the case had begun to solidify. She was anxious to share her idea.

Wes entered the room just behind Ben. "Hey," he said briefly to her, then crossed to the recycling bin to toss out his beer bottle. "Want another one?" he asked his brother.

Now how in the world could he act so nonchalant around her when she got a head rush and butterflies colliding in her stomach when she so much as glanced his way?

"Yeah," Ben said as he set the platter of steaks on the counter.

Monica handed her a glass of champagne, and Cara resisted the urge to slug down half the contents. Why did the guy make her feel so unsettled? It was damn annoying.

Sipping her drink, she watched him wander over to the cupola and stare out the window. Even in a crowd he seemed to be alone. She knew the feeling well and wondered if he just wasn't a people person, or if he, like her, pushed people away for deeper reasons. After so many years in foster homes, she tended to keep people at a distance out of a lack of trust and an awkwardness about sharing her feelings. Did he feel the same?

Monica had once shared with her the circumstances of Ben and Wes's father's death. She'd also said that their mother had fallen apart after he'd passed away and now lived in Florida. Apparently their mom rarely saw or spoke to her children. Maybe Wes felt abandoned. Cara sensed a kindred spirit, and that seemed like a really bad thing in the middle of a major case.

Looking away from him, she leaned against the center island. "Do we have to make small talk first, or can we get right to the case?"

Ben's gaze went directly to Monica.

She heaved a sigh. "Can we at least wait until after dinner for the gruesome details?"

Cara figured she was being rude, but with Wes around she felt especially awkward. She kept having flashbacks to her first double date, which had been forced upon her by one of her foster sisters. Everyone had laughed and talked as they ate pizza, while she'd been so frozen into silence the guys had thought she didn't speak English. Not exactly her finest moment.

To talk you had to share pieces of yourself, reveal feelings and ambitions. Too personal. Too close. People she got close to always left her—one way or another.

As the group took their places at the table, she shook off the loneliness. Those days were gone. She made her own decisions, spent time with the people she wanted to.

And she admitted—if only to herself—Wes Kimball was one of those people.

Dammit.

DURING DINNER, Cara put her theory on hold, mentioned the house, and Monica pretty much took care of the conversation. But she couldn't avoid the stoic Lieutenant Kimball. Probably because he sat right next to her.

His thigh nearly touched hers.

Their hands even brushed once.

He barely spoke. He grunted. And ate. Occasionally, he sipped beer.

She'd never been so intensely aware of a man before. (Though she could have done without the grunting.) She smelled his cologne over the steak. She found herself staring at his hand as he brought his fork to his mouth. Even listening to Monica describe paint colors and installing tile, Cara knew the moment he moved his hand.

As they dug into dessert—a multilayered chocolate brownie that Cara nearly had an orgasm over—all thoughts of work flew the coop. She was wondering if Monica had actually produced this incredible culinary creation with her own hands when Ben said, "Wes, you mentioned at the station that Addison wasn't anxious to solve the case. What did you mean by that?"

Still in the throes of chocolate ecstasy, it took Cara a few moments to realize Ben was speaking of their earlier conversation with the mayor.

Wes set down his fork.

Cara marveled at the willpower of this man.

Wes's gaze flicked to his brother, then he glanced at Cara—the first time all night, by her estimation. He leaned back. "I think Addison is responsible for these fires. He's hired someone to set them to collect the insurance money."

Cara said nothing. She'd known from the moment they'd discussed Addison how Wes had felt about him. And since his theory didn't completely contradict hers, she felt comfortable waiting for her own moment.

Ben rubbed his chin. "That's a quick judgment. And it has a big problem—Addison's loaded."

"He *appears* loaded. But I've heard people talking about him doing a lot of gambling, taking lots of trips to Vegas. God knows he throws his money around town like crazy." He leaned forward, his blue eyes blazing as he tapped the table with his finger. "Who knows what we'll find if we dig deep enough?"

Silence followed this accusation. Cara had investigated enough cases to realize Robert Addison was an untouchable. One of the beautiful, wealthy people who didn't have to explain their actions or take responsibility for their mistakes. That didn't mean she wouldn't go after him if the evidence dictated, but it certainly made things sticky. And she didn't have to live in this town afterward.

Monica rose. "I'll start cleaning up and let you—"

Standing, Ben wrapped his hand around her wrist. "It'll keep. I want to hear your opinion." He kissed her palm, then pulled her back down into her chair.

Though her mind had managed to move from chocolate to arson, Cara couldn't help but smile inwardly at their display of affection. She'd heard a lot about Ben from her friend and sensed the love they had for one another, but seeing the reality made even her cynical heart sigh.

Monica ran her finger around the rim of her champagne glass. "Addison is charming enough."

"But..." Cara added for her.

"I don't like him," Monica said flatly, flipping her long hair over her shoulder.

Ben tossed his napkin onto his plate. "There's a lot of that going around."

"Sorry, honey." Monica laid her hand over her husband's. "Most women adore him, of course. He's loaded, good-looking, generous. But he's too cocky. Like everybody should worship at his feet. Always has to be the center of attention. Now I like being the center of attention as much as anybody..."

"But, darling, you don't have to try," Ben said, gripping her hand and pulling her closer to him.

"Do you guys need some time alone?" Wes asked dryly. "'Cause Cara and I can go."

"Sorry." With obvious effort, Ben let go of his wife. "I guess I'm going to have to take this character assassination of Addison seriously—much as it's going to cause me grief. I don't ever remember you and Wes agreeing about anything.

"But," he continued, "it would certainly make my life easier if Addison was innocent. Cara, I half hope you fall head over heels for the man."

Cara raised her eyebrows. "Don't count on it."

Monica laughed and rose from the table, carrying her plate toward the sink. "Go right on wishing, Chief, honey. Cara isn't easily moved—especially by men."

Ben got up from the table, as well. "She's here to help me with a case, darling, I doubt she wants comments made about her personal life."

Cara stood to help clear the table. Wes rose, too, and to Cara's surprise eased Monica out of the way, rolled up his sleeves, then proceeded to rinse the dishes.

Just a few feet from Wes's broad back, Cara leaned against the island. "Oh, she's not talking about anything personal."

Monica smiled at her. "Actually, I was talking about this guy Cara and the police arrested about a month ago. He tried to escape as she was putting him in handcuffs."

Ben took a plate from Wes and loaded it into the dishwasher. "What did you do?" he asked, looking as if he wasn't too sure he wanted to know.

She shrugged. "Kneed him in the balls."

Wes coughed. A plate clattered in the sink.

Ben slapped his brother on the back. "Don't worry. I'm sure she's more easygoing with colleagues."

Cara said nothing.

Monica laughed.

The two men exchanged a worried look, then Ben cleared his throat. "Well...why don't we head into the den? Cara can tell us her ideas. We might even have this whole thing wrapped up by the late news."

Cara shook her head. "I wouldn't count on it." She paused, then smiled. "Chief, honey."

WES SHIFTED in his brother's recliner and watched Cara pace in front of the fireplace.

Her energy was fascinating, though not contagious. He was perfectly comfortable studying her, quietly wondering what made her tick, gripping the recliner's armrests as he wrestled with the desire simmering through his veins.

Damn, he had it bad.

Though what "it" was exactly, he had no idea.

"Since I haven't met Mr. Addison, or completed the investigation into his lifestyle and finances, I'm reserving judgment about whether or not he's involved in the arson." She stopped suddenly, then rolled her shoulders back and looked directly at him. "I think it's likely a professional set the fires."

Wes didn't budge his gaze from hers. She agreed with him—at least on the professional angle. A rare feeling of acceptance rolled through him, warming him down to his toes.

"Addison isn't the only person in town capable of hiring a professional," Ben pointed out from his position next to Monica on the sofa.

"Naturally," Cara said, resuming her pacing. "Let's start with the first fire—with what we know. Our perp dismantles the sprinkler system, then sets the fire using gasoline. Why? Obviously, so the building is destroyed. But he leaves the phone system intact. So when the smoke detectors trigger the security system, here comes the fire department."

"Maybe he didn't realize that," Monica said.

"Mmm. My assumption, as well, when Ben initially sent me the file. Guy screwed up, got nervous, or maybe he just doesn't know his way around sprinkler and fire alarm systems very well. Then, of course, there's always the possibility we're dealing with a prankster—or a nut. A pyromaniac. They like the attention and *want* the fire to be discovered. If the media comes all the better."

"We don't have much media in Baxter, though," Ben pointed out. "Just a local, weekly newspaper."

"Who I bet will run a special edition in the morning—'Arsonist at Large in Baxter!'" Wes said.

He could see where Cara was going, at least partly. He'd been a cop long enough to understand that for some people the crime was just a means to an end. They liked the excitement, danger and publicity that came with breaking the law. From cat burglars to serial killers, these people were an odd, sometimes highly disturbed group that were all the harder to catch for the seeming randomness of their crimes.

He'd been thinking of this case one-dimensionally. Addison's need for money led him to set the fires, or hire someone to do it for him. Fire equals much-needed cash. But Cara's insight forced him to realize even a simply motivated crime could be complex. The person who set the fires was the key, even if he was a hired gun. Understanding the psyche of this person would lead to his arrest.

"The newspaper," Cara said, waving her hand. "We'll get to more of that. Now, we have a second fire. All the old theories go out the window. By definition, we're dealing with a serial arsonist. And one who seems to be in a hurry. Two fires, two weeks.

"So, we get to those details. Again, the guy—I'm calling him a guy generically, of course. This could be a woman, though the statistics don't support that. The guy comes with his can of gasoline. Again the sprinkler system is dismantled. But this time, he cuts the lines from the smoke detector to the alarm. Why? He'd learned from the first fire, you might say."

"But you don't say," Ben said.

"I don't *think*." She shrugged but kept pacing. "It's just a theory. Anyway, our arsonist has cut the lines from the smoke detector to the phones—in the warehouse. No alarms. No sprinklers. The system can't contact the fire department. But then he does a very curious thing."

"He sets the trash can in the office on fire," Wes put in.

"Exactly. Fire heats up, set off the sprinklers in there, and in minutes the fire department arrives."

Monica frowned. "That seems pretty stupid."

"And risky," Ben added. "The warehouse was nearly a complete loss. He had to have hung around while that burned, then set the fire in the office just before he left."

Cara stopped and turned toward them. "More exciting, though, isn't it?"

Wes suddenly realized he was right before in guessing Cara's theory. This guy wasn't a garden-variety fire starter. He wondered if Addison realized he'd hired a nut. "He *wanted* the fire department there."

"I think so," Cara said as she walked toward him. "I spent this morning reading newspaper coverage of the first fire, and I found a line that intrigued me." She pulled a piece of newspaper from her back pocket then handed it to Wes. "Read the highlighted part."

Wes found the spot and read, "'The arsonist didn't do the whole job; however, the security system alerted the fire department, who heroically arrived to contain the blaze.'"

"He didn't like that—who are all these lousy firefighters, getting all my press? So, he makes a riskier move the second time. He waited around to make sure the warehouse burned to the ground so there would be nothing left for the firefighters to do, nothing to save. He wanted to prove to us he knew how to do it."

"That's cocky," Monica said. "Sounds like he'll be easy to catch."

Wes's gaze slid from Cara to Monica, then back. That crazy redhead just loved to push people's buttons.

Cara's eyes flashed briefly, then she rocked back on her heels. "Could be."

Ben rose, tunneling his hand through his hair. "Sounds like he's going to be a pain in the butt to me."

"And dangerous," Wes added. "He's already killed one person."

"Inadvertently, I think," Cara said, her gaze going to Wes's, and the sight of her standing over that horrible death scene again flickered through his mind. "But yes."

"So where do we begin?" Ben asked.

For the first time since the fire, Wes realized how hard this whole thing would be on all of them—especially his brother. Since Dad's death, Ben had taken on the burdens and worries of the entire family. He'd become their leader, and sometimes their pain-in-the-butt surrogate parent. Since their mom had lost the strength for rules and discipline, the task had fallen to Ben.

As a teenager, Wes had resented the hell out of him. As an adult, he acknowledged he had no right to criticize a responsibility he'd never have taken on himself.

He knew Ben would blame himself for these disasters. He'd feel compelled to run interference between Wes and the mayor as the case progressed. He'd accept responsibility and rise to the challenge of leadership, just as he always had. Wes didn't want to cause his brother more grief. He just always seemed to find himself standing on the other side of popular opinion.

"The evidence crew found a pair of half-burned latex gloves in the trash can. There's not much left, but they're hopeful. They're sending the sample to the state lab tomorrow. I've also compiled a list of all the people who've had altercations with Mr. Addison in the last six months," she continued.

"Must be a long list," Wes said.

She raised her eyebrows. "And I'm sure you won't mind helping me go through it."

He smiled. "Love to."

"Go easy, Wes," Ben said in his best Chief Big Shot tone.

Wes ignored the jab of disappointment to his gut. He might not meet his brother's expectations, but he wasn't an idiot. "And I was so looking forward to torturing the townsfolk." He rose. "I gotta go."

"Me, too." Cara shook Ben's hand, hugged Monica, then they all walked to the foyer.

"It's late," Ben said as he opened the door. "Wes, why don't you follow Cara back to her apartment?"

He'd already planned to do that. How did his brother always manage to make him feel like a naughty five-year-old? "Sure."

"I'm a big girl, guys," Cara said, sliding into her leather jacket.

Ben angled his head. "Please. I'd feel better."

Cara shrugged. "Thanks again for dinner."

"Anytime," Monica said, catching her friend's gaze. "And we should get together for lunch this week."

"I'm going to be neck-deep in this case, but I'll try."

Wes had a hard time picturing Cara and Monica at Belle's Café, with Cara in her leather jacket and sidearm, sipping iced tea and sitting across from Monica in her flashy miniskirt and four-inch stilettos.

After they said their goodbyes, he and Cara climbed into their vehicles, and he followed her to her apartment complex. He parked his truck next to her car, then strode behind her up the stairs to the second floor.

She didn't say anything. Her brow was furrowed as if she was concentrating and not even aware he was there.

It had been a wild twenty-four hours—really not even that long—so he supposed distraction was easy to come by.

He was distracted, as well. Not by the case, but by the gentle sway of her backside as she climbed the stairs. Damn, she was beautiful. Though he realized she wasn't movie-star perfect, those remarkable eyes of hers, her energy and dedication to her job, and the woman he sensed lurking beneath the investigator had captivated him.

Not a good idea, Lieutenant.

He was already on both his brother's and the mayor's watch list. And as much as Ben's stuffy, superior attitude pissed him off at times, he'd spent too many years yearning for his brother's approval to quell that desire now.

And he was nearly positive that sleeping with a colleague during a case would be on everybody's no-no list.

"How about we meet at the station at ten?" he suggested when they reached her door.

She cut her gaze toward him. "Try eight."

"I won't be happy at eight."

"Then you can be the bad cop."

He liked her toughness, even as he wanted to find her gentleness. He had to fight to control his breathing, clench his hands to keep from reaching out. Thoughts of Ben and the mayor retreated. He'd never been much for no-no lists or following the rules. "Do I get to carry your gun?"

"Nobody touches my gun." She turned to unlock her door, then glanced back over her shoulder. "Eight sharp."

"Yes, ma'am." His face was only inches from her. Heat rolled off her body, and he couldn't miss the flare of interest in her sea-green eyes.

Without thinking, he captured her mouth with his, sliding his tongue past her lips, wrapping his arms around her waist and pulling her body against his.

She moaned and thrust her arms around his neck.

Her body was an intriguing combination of hard muscle and womanly softness. That tough look in her eyes, the hard set of her jaw were part of her, tools of intimidation to keep people away, but she also yielded to him without reservation, as if wanting to absorb the sensations that touched her very soul. Why she was allowing him to handle her, he had no idea. He didn't care.

As he continued to explore her lips, he crushed her body against his, her rounded breasts pressing against his chest, his erection pressing against her stomach. He clenched his hands at her waist, backing her against the door, holding her in place with his hips. His erection throbbed in response. The sensation was both relief and torture.

He wanted more, to give into the clawing hunger, but he didn't want to let her go long enough to open the door. Fire burned in his belly, seeming to stream heat between the two of them.

She tore her mouth from his. "We have to stop."

Chest heaving, saying nothing, he fought to gain control of his body.

"I don't do this with colleagues," she added.

He didn't have any female colleagues, but he'd met a woman and slept with her in the same night before. Though, for some reason, he didn't want to admit that to Cara. "Okay," he said, letting go of her and stepping back.

Blood still roared through his head, but he forced his desire to chill.

Cara stared at him with a shocked, wide-eyed expression that reflected his own slammed-upside-the-head feelings. She rolled her shoulders. "I'm sorry. I don't know what got into me." She shrugged. "Exhaustion, I guess."

He didn't care for that justification and didn't believe it for a second. Whatever this wild attraction was between them, it fed off hunger and heat, not cold exhaustion.

"Well, forget it ever happened, okay?" she continued. "We have to work together, after all, and I need to concentrate on this case. I'm sure you have plenty of women lining up to…" She pressed her lips together, and he could have sworn she blushed.

He leaned one shoulder against the door. "I think that's the most you've ever said at one time that didn't involve the case."

"I'm not much of a talker."

"You're a woman."

She glared at him. "Good night, Lieutenant."

He smiled and brushed a strand of hair off her face. "But I was just about to let you cut to the front of the line."

4

CARA STARED UP into the confident face of Wes Kimball. "The *front* of the line? Aren't I lucky?"

His grin only widened. "Let me inside. We could both get lucky."

She crossed her arms over her chest. "That's original."

In truth, he was way too damn appealing. His bright blue eyes and dangerous smile. And those lips. Sensual and soft, with the edge of his goatee tickling her face. The man could *kiss.* Oh, yeah, loads of heat and passion lurked inside the volatile lieutenant, waiting to explode, daring someone to tap beneath the surface.

Not that she had any intention of exploring.

"You're going to deny how good we'd be together?"

"Yes."

He seemed surprised by her direct answer. "Why?"

"I don't get involved with colleagues."

"Technically, you're my boss."

"Sort of. Really, Ben is." She sighed. "Are you always this difficult?"

"Yes."

She bit the inside of her cheek to keep from smiling. "Look, it's nothing personal. I work almost exclusively with men. I'm outnumbered, so I'm a curiosity to some, a challenge to others." She didn't think Wes fell into either of these categories, but she watched his reaction carefully anyway. "I also don't sleep around, and I won't compromise my reputation or professionalism for a couple of hours of horizontal fun."

He said nothing for a moment, then his eyes darkened. He leaned closer. "We could do it vertically."

Her mouth went dry. The masculine, spicy scent of his cologne literally made her head light. A vision of them with him cupping her backside, her braced against the door, while he—

She cut off her thoughts. "I'm sure you could," she managed to say.

His gaze searched her face. "But not with you."

"Not with me." *Not tonight.*

Excuse me, Miss Professional? Try not ever.

He shrugged as if he got turned down all the time—which she doubted—or as if he made an offer to every woman just for the hell of it. *That* she could believe.

"So eight o'clock tomorrow?" he asked.

She nodded. "We'll start on our list of people who've had conflicts with Addison."

"That's good. We ought to be done by next Christmas."

She ignored his comment. "Then we'll finish up with the man himself."

His gaze shot to hers. "You're interviewing Addison tomorrow?"

"At four o'clock. His office."

"I want to be there."

Arrogant and demanding to the core. But then she was, too, so she respected those qualities. Besides, she'd already planned to have him there. "You want to be the good cop or the bad cop?"

He leaned toward her, his eyes sliding easily from business to pleasure. "What do you think?"

She swallowed. *Okay. Mark the lieutenant down as bad cop.*

Bad for her piece of mind, bad for her concentration. But he could be good for her body. Maybe—

"Who do we see first?"

She blinked, trying to recall her first appointment. She had to check her PDA.

Bad for my memory, too.

She finally found her appointments. "We've got Roland Patterson, owner of the pet shop—"

"Holy hell."

"What's wrong with Patterson?"

Wes sighed. "Nothing. It's nothing."

She resisted the urge to grab him by the front of his shirt and shake the information out of him. "If you have details about one of our subjects, Lieutenant, I expect you to share them with me."

His face flushed, but all he said was "You'll see" as he turned and stalked away.

WES DROPPED his keys on the kitchen counter in his house and headed to the fridge for a soda. He chugged half the contents, then walked into the living room.

As he dropped into his recliner, he considered turning on the TV, but he knew he wouldn't find anything he liked. He was exhausted, yet his brain buzzed.

From long habit, his gaze slid to the mantel. He stared at the ancient, brass-framed picture of his family, taken just months before his father had died. The senseless death of the homeless man and Wes's worries about his and Ben's relationship weighed heavy on his mind, so the questions came.

If Dad had lived, would Wes be a different man? Would injustice anger him as much? Would the loneliness he couldn't seem to shake never have overwhelmed him in the first place?

As for his relationship with Ben, he knew he could try harder. He knew how much his brother valued professionalism. Wes could help by at least conforming in some areas, by holding back his frustration with Mayor Collins and trying to be open-minded about Addison's guilt. Since he really didn't see that last one happening, he should probably concentrate on the other two—at least until this case was over, and he could find a way to talk to Ben about their lack of closeness.

He probably needed to find some restraint where Cara was concerned, as well. He'd shrugged off her rejection earlier, but inside he'd wanted to argue, to press his point about their attraction.

And he had the feeling that when he saw her again his control would slip away. Reasoning and promises of restraint would be forgotten. Women were usually a distraction, a release, a part of his life he didn't have to share with his job. But his fascination with Cara didn't seem nearly that simple, and not just because she *was* part of his job.

Since he knew he wasn't solving that deal anytime soon, he turned off the light, tossed out his empty can, then headed upstairs to his bedroom. He needed to get some sleep. The interviews with Patterson and Addison tomorrow would undoubtedly require a well of patience he didn't even begin to have.

"MR. PATTERSON, I'm over here," Cara said, waving at their interview subject.

The flushed pet store owner dragged his gaze from Wes.

Cara just rolled her eyes.

It had been going on like this ever since she and Wes arrived at the pet store fifteen minutes ago. Usually, she was the attraction—or at least the oddity—in an interview. But Wes—clad casually in worn blue jeans and a tan button-up shirt, his hair still damp from his morning shower—had commanded Roland Patterson's attention instantly. A fact the lieutenant must not care for, considering the way he squirmed in his seat in front of Patterson's desk.

Obviously, they needed to switch roles.

She fixed a steely glare on their subject. "Mr. Patterson, about this incident with Robert Addison. We're going to give you a chance to tell your side, but you'd better justify to me pretty damn quickly why I shouldn't put your name at the top of my suspect list for these arsons."

Patterson's mouth formed an *O*. "I'm a suspect?"

"Yes." She didn't for a second think he was guilty, but maybe the gravity of the situation would finally hit the man.

Patterson smiled, his brown eyes twinkling. "If I don't answer will you interrogate me under hot lights?"

What? "No."

"What about good cop-bad cop?"

Since they were already doing that, Cara was at a loss for words. She glanced at Wes. He shook his head and rubbed his temples.

"How about Chinese water torture?"

Cara jumped to her feet, leaning over Patterson's desk. "You've got about ten seconds to start taking this interview seriously, or—"

"You'll haul me downtown?" Patterson all but bounced in his seat in excitement.

With effort, Cara swallowed the urge to grab Patterson by his throat. She dropped back in her chair and extended her hand toward Wes in a he's-all-yours gesture.

Seemingly full of sincerity, Wes leaned back in his chair, propping one booted foot on his knee. "Mr. Patterson, why don't you just tell us about the incident that occurred on August fifteenth at Mr. Addison's home?"

Patterson huffed and sighed, but he finally got down to business. "That wretched man."

"Addison?" Wes supplied, only too happily.

"Yes, Robert Addison. He'd bought a dog from me—a gorgeous chocolate lab with big brown eyes. A sensitive soul."

A *dog* with a sensitive soul? How did he know? Cara shook her head and vowed deeper concentration on the pieces of the story that were actually relevant.

"On the fifteenth Addison called me to his house," Patterson continued, "demanding I take the dog back and give him a refund because the dog had—" he lowered his voice "—done his business on Addison's Persian rug."

"This was a grown dog or a puppy?" Wes asked.

"He was just a puppy!" Patterson cried. "So I go out there and learn—from the servants, mind you—he hasn't taken any time with the pup. He's made no effort to train him or show him the door where he's supposed to go out. He hasn't used the kenneling technique I told him would be best, because the kennel *ruined the ambiance* of the den. The staff had tried to help, but between their own duties and Mr. Addison's constant shouting…well, it was a mess."

"And this is what led to the assault?" Cara asked.

Patterson rolled his eyes. "Assault, my ass. I slapped him, and considering the rumors about his sexual proclivities…"

"Let's stick to the facts, rather than rumors," Wes said, again shifting in his seat.

What sexual proclivities? Cara wondered. She hadn't caught wind of this. *Please not another sicko.* Sometimes she felt as if she were wading hip-deep in them.

"Why did you slap him?" Wes asked, still displaying an odd sort of calm, considering how passionately negative he felt about Addison.

Patterson rolled his shoulders. A light of pure hatred lit his eyes. "When I tried to pick up the little pup, he flinched."

Cara's stomach sank. She'd seen—though thankfully only a few times—kids in the state orphan system with the same reaction. As if they didn't recognize kindness when they saw it.

"He'd beaten the dog," Wes said on a sigh.

"Yes," Patterson said tightly. "He's lucky I didn't do the same to him."

OUTSIDE the pet shop, Cara stuffed her hands into her jacket pockets and watched the easy flow of traffic down Main Street. The trees in the park across the street had turned varying shades of yellow, orange and red. Shoppers strolled on the sidewalk. A kid licked a big, colorful sucker while he held his mommy's hand.

Even in small, quiet Baxter ugliness existed. She'd met killers who didn't beat their dog.

It was enough to depress the hell out of a person.

"Patterson's smart enough," she said to Wes. "Certainly angry enough."

"Smart? You call threatening a subject in the presence of two investigators smart?"

Cara smiled slightly. She enjoyed sparring with the lieutenant. "Maybe intelligent is a better word. He could have researched security and sprinkler systems."

Wes glanced at her, his eyes as bright as the blue sky hovering above them. He really was amazing to look at. Not slick or designer, like so many men in Atlanta. But real. And strong. Maybe even hard.

"I don't see him as our guy," he said. "Patterson's temper is hot. This perp's anger is calculated and cold, ice-cold."

"Addison again."

"It fits. The whole thing fits him to a *T*. His need to show everybody he's smarter than the cops. He likes doing the research and he likes even better exposing himself to the danger."

"How about if at least one of us stays objective?"

He leaned toward her, his jaw tight. "I'm telling you he's guilty. It's him."

The heat of anger that poured off him only made him that much more appealing, but she still found his prejudice appalling. "Maybe we should just skip the investigative process, arrest him and toss him in jail." She paused, but he only glared at her. "Or we could just circumvent the entire judicial system, get an angry mob together and hang him from the tallest tree in the park."

Wes extended his hand. "Lead on."

"Working your usual charms on the ladies?" asked an annoyed female voice from behind Cara.

Turning, Cara saw a tiny blonde tapping her foot and glaring in Wes's direction. She was as light as he was dark, but she had the Kimball baby blues, and having met her recently when she'd visited Atlanta with Monica, the practicality that the opinionated lieutenant lacked.

"This guy giving you trouble?" Skyler Kimball Tesson asked.

"Nothing I can't handle."

Skyler smiled. "I'm sure."

Wes crossed his arms over his chest. "We don't have time to chat, Sky. We're investigating a case."

Cara cut her gaze in his direction. "I thought we were recruiting a lynch mob. Skyler's small, but she's tough, I bet."

Wes looked at his watch. "Our next appointment is in fifteen minutes. Do you want to go or not?"

Skyler's glance darted from her brother to Cara then back. She smiled even wider this time. Cara could all but see the wheels of speculation turning in her mind.

"Going," she said quickly. "Bye, Skyler." She didn't need Wes's sister adding to the side of her that ridiculously wanted to give into the searing attraction between her and Wes.

"Don't be a stranger, Cara," Skyler called after them. "We'll have lunch."

"Sure," Cara called back, not pausing as she strode toward Wes's truck.

That innocent-looking woman had had a definite hand in getting Monica and Ben together. She'd even given Monica advice when she'd dated Wes. And while Skyler seemed to be batting five hundred with Monica, Cara wanted no part of her matchmaking or a long-term relationship.

She glanced at Wes as he started the truck. Even a guy with very capable-looking hands.

Nope, nope, nope. Loner she'd always been. Loner she'd remain.

Who says he has any long-term plans? Wes, the rebel, hotheaded troublemaker isn't a forever kind of guy. Right? Probably.

But he's a colleague.

A *temporary* colleague.

"She's up to something," Wes said as he pulled away from the curb.

Cara nearly choked on her tongue. "Who?"

"Skyler. Did you see that weird look she gave me? And that smile?"

Cara, of course, had seen the same thing, but she wanted to deal with Skyler on her own. She had to stop the wheels from turning ASAP. She didn't have the time or patience for romance.

"I didn't notice," she said to Wes and turned her head to stare out the window.

AT 3:55 P.M., Wes held open Addison's office door for Cara.

They'd learned little over the past few hours. Ten more interviews—none of them nearly as whacked or entertaining as Roland Patterson's—and they'd gotten anger, tears and empty threats. Two former lovers who weren't excited about the former part. Three former employees, also not much on the "former." No one seemed competent or steady-handed enough to pull off two arsons.

And all day long he'd had to smell *her*, sit next to *her*, watch her stormy eyes go from patient understanding to cold steel as each suspect and witness was questioned. His prediction from last night was coming true.

He was absolutely on the edge of losing it.

"Will you sit down?" she whispered, glancing at the secretary a few feet away. "We need to stay in control here."

Not even aware of his pacing, Wes dropped into the chair next to her. The scent of gardenias brushed by him. It was such an ultrafeminine, sweet smell—and at odds with the image he had of the tough captain—he found himself longing to lean forward, inhale more, absorb more.

But he ground his teeth together, resisting. Control was going down fast.

"Do you remember the routine?" Cara asked, her breath teasing the side of his neck.

He clamped down on his libido. "I sit silently, looking angry and stern while you sweetly ask him the questions."

"Go with me—no matter what. I think he'll be more cooperative with a woman."

"I'm sure." Past moments, where he'd witnessed Addison working his charms on women in bars, restaurants and around town, rolled through his mind. The guy was smooth, no doubt about it. Then he had an image of Cara and Addison in a teasing, intimate conversation, and he found himself grinding his teeth again. Stupid. As long as Addison finally got some retribution handed to him what difference did it make how that happened?

"Maybe I should just go, then you can invite him to your place for dinner."

Obviously annoyed, she stared at him. "'*The ladies seem to like him*'—your exact words. It's a good investigative strategy. Why are you getting your jock all twisted about this?"

Wes forced himself to think like a cop, rather than a man. He had no personal connection to Cara. Her proximity to Addison shouldn't matter to him.

So, why did it?

"Just realize ninety-nine percent of what he says is crap," he said.

"*This* is why I want you to be quiet. I'm capable of forming my own opinions, you know."

"I just—"

"Mr. Addison will see you now," the secretary announced, rising from her chair.

As she led them down a dark-gray-carpeted hallway, Wes glanced at his watch. Fifteen minutes Addison had kept them waiting. A not-so-subtle clue that he wasn't worried about what they'd ask and considered this meeting an inconvenience to his busy schedule. Most suspects and interviewees started sweating the moment the appointment was set, so they were usually a wreck by the time the cops arrived.

Wes would bet his truck's new mag wheels that ice cubes wouldn't melt on Addison's butt in the dead of summer. A small detail like double arson and manslaughter wasn't likely to affect him too much either.

Addison rose from behind his sleek, charcoal-gray marble desk as they walked in, then—all smiles—walked casually toward them. "Wes Kimball, isn't it?" he asked, shaking Wes's hand and angling his head as if he couldn't quite place him.

Simply nodding, Wes dropped into a chair in front of Addison's desk.

Addison's gaze locked on Cara. His brown eyes danced with warmth. "And you must be Captain Hughes."

Cara's face lit with such a warm, sexy smile, Wes blinked in shock. "Call me Cara," she said as she blushed—actually *blushed*—and shook Addison's hand.

"And I'm Robbie."

Wes was pretty damn sure he was going to puke. She hadn't even let *him* call her by her first name.

"We just have a few questions, Mr. A— I mean, Robbie. I'm sure you're a very busy man."

"I have plenty of time for such an important investigation. I understand a man lost his life in the fire."

He shook his head with regret. "Awful. Has his family been located? I'd like to contact them."

"No family we know of. He appears to be a homeless man who wandered in to get out of the cold."

Addison sighed dramatically. "Tragic."

Oh, please.

Cara glanced around the opulent office, her gaze pausing on the rows of shadow-boxed footballs. "Did you play?"

Tragedy obviously dismissed, Addison's smile widened. "Quarterback, University of Georgia. I was all-conference two years in a row."

"Really?"

Wes resisted the urge to roll his eyes. Gee, it took a real detective to figure *that* one out, what with the whole office decorated in black and red and every inch of wall space covered by dozens of framed pictures featuring golden boy in his athletic prime.

Let her roll with it, he told himself. *Stick to the plan.*

Still, he glared at them over his shoulder.

After several long minutes of shameless gushing over Addison's athletic prowess, Cara finally caught his gaze. She flushed again. "Oh, my. I guess we really should get these questions out of the way."

"You think we should?" Wes asked, thankfully not having to hide his sarcasm.

Addison seemed reluctant to leave his favorite subject, but had little choice when Cara crossed the room and sank into the chair next to Wes. With her back to their suspect, she winked at Wes.

The gesture reminded him that she was playing a part and not likely to fall at blond-haired, blue-eyed, pretty boy Addison's feet anytime soon. It also gave him the encouragement to intensify his hard stare.

Cara couldn't be taking Addison seriously. This was a man who'd had track lighting installed above his desk to emphasize the highlights in his *hair.*

Cara reached into her inside jacket pocket. "So..."

Wes half hoped she'd pull out her gun—*that* would put a crimp in Mr. Cocky's smile—but of course she'd locked her pistol in the glove compartment of his truck. *Wouldn't want to scare the innocent suspect, now would we?*

Cara pulled out a wire-bound notebook, flipping it open as if she needed a moment to gather her thoughts.

Addison slid into his black leather executive chair, folded his manicured hands in front of him and smiled indulgently. "So...here we are."

What an asshole.

Cara glanced up and pretended—at least Wes assumed she was pretending—she was flustered by his undivided attention. "Right." Another blush. "Well...first off I guess I should ask where you were at the times of the fires."

Addison blinked at the abrupt question.

Wes couldn't resist smiling at his partner. No gentle lead-in, no apology for his loss, no assurances that they were going to get the lousy SOB who destroyed his property. *This* was an interrogation he could get into.

In keeping with her clueless-little-me persona, though, she immediately let her jaw drop open. "Oh, gosh. That was a little forward, wasn't it? I'm so sorry. I just have this list." She tapped her notebook. "I have to do everything in order, so I don't get confused."

Addison's smile returned. "Of course."

"Okay, now, I guess we could start with question number two." She pulled out the ballpoint pen stuffed in the notebook's wire ring. "You had insurance on the office and the warehouse, didn't you?"

"Yes. Naturally, all my properties are insured."

She stared at her notebook, clicking her pen. "And how much would those amounts be?"

Addison's eyes narrowed for a second, then he cleared his throat. "The real estate office is four hundred thousand, and the warehouse is just over two million, including inventory."

"And was the warehouse full of inventory?"

"There are always some items moving in and out," Addison said vaguely.

"How about a percentage?" Wes asked, his gaze pining the other man's.

"Seventy."

As Cara glanced at Wes, he could envision the wheels turning in her brain. Addison hadn't checked his files, called his secretary or even looked at the notepad on his desk. He *knew* the capacity.

Cara made notes. "Insurance company giving you any trouble?" she asked almost absently. When Addison didn't immediately respond, she looked up. "Any trouble, Robbie?"

"Naturally, they need clearance from your office before releasing any payments. I spoke with my claims adjustor yesterday and this morning."

Interesting. The last fire had occurred less than forty-eight hours ago, and he'd already spoken with the insurance company twice. *Anxious, are you, buddy?*

Cara flushed again. "Oh, right. We'll get this little matter cleared up ASAP."

Was that relief that danced through Addison's eyes? Wes fought to keep his slumped pose, wondering if Cara was right. Had his personal experiences with Addison so colored his judgment that he couldn't even read the suspect's reactions accurately?

Addison shrugged. "No rush. I want to make sure the investigation is thorough."

"Of course." Cara glanced at her notebook, then back at him. "Now, back to my first question. Could you tell me where you were both last week on the night of the first fire and the night before last? I know it's awkward, but I have to put it in my report...."

Good grief, the woman was a female Columbo. All she needed was a cigar and a rumpled tan raincoat.

Addison held up his hand as if he intended to stay any more excuses. "It's all right, really. It's just—Well, the information needs to be handled delicately. Discreetly."

"Oh, Robbie, you can count on me."

"I was with a woman."

"All night? Both nights?"

"Until 6:00 a.m. the first time, then, this past Tuesday until I was paged at 1:30 a.m."

"Oh." Cara's cheeks went pink. "I see."

"I wouldn't want anyone to think I was bragging or anything..."

Now Wes did roll his eyes. He shifted impatiently in his chair. But of course neither Addison nor Cara looked his way. They were too wrapped up in each other.

Go with me—no matter what, she'd said. A bigger challenge than he'd thought.

"Of course not." Smiling, Cara leaned forward. "Now, what was the lady in question's name? For my file, you know."

Addison cleared his throat. "Actually that would be lad*ies.*"

Oh, please. Wes glanced at Cara to see if she was buying any of this fake modesty.

"During the first fire, I had dinner with one woman, then about midnight I went to another woman's house. I stayed there all night. The night before last, I did the same thing, except I didn't stay the entire evening."

"Mmm," she said, staring at her notebook. "I guess we should move on, then."

Wes looked pointedly at her. *No, we shouldn't,* he wanted to say. Push him. Who are these women? Addison for sure wasn't trying to protect anybody's reputation, which Wes knew from personal experience. When Addison moved on a woman, he usually made sure half the town knew. So, unless Robbie the Discreet was screwing the mayor's wife, Wes didn't see why they should let him off.

Go with me... Wes held on to his opinions—by a thread.

"What about enemies, Robbie? Who do you think is targeting you?" Cara asked quietly.

Addison spread his hands wide. "I'm honestly not sure. A man doesn't get where I am without making a few enemies along the way, I guess. But I haven't received any threats or anything like that. It could be a former employee, I suppose. The fire department called here for that list last week, I believe."

"Yes, we received it. I'm in the process of interviewing those people now."

All sincerity, Addison fixed his gaze on Cara's face. His expression was warm, his eyes intent. "I'm afraid I run a large company. I'm sorry to have to put you through so much work in investigating."

"It's okay. That's my job." She paused, continuing to stare into Addison's eyes for another moment or two.

Wes gripped the arms of his chair.

"Well, I guess that's everything." Cara flipped her notebook closed, then rose, shaking Addison's hand. "Thanks so much for your time. And you'll let us know if you think of anybody who might hold a grudge against you, won't you?"

Addison stood, holding Cara's hand intimately between his. "Of course. You'll update me, as well?"

She smiled and extended a business card. "Of course." She turned without looking at Wes and headed toward the door. Like an obedient puppy, he followed her. Though he knew the entire interview had been a charade, his temper was ready to surface anyway.

When he walked around her to open the door, she looked back at Addison. "Oh, and can I get you to call my office in the morning with those ladies' names?" She smiled at him over her shoulder. "I promise to be discreet. Thanks so much." She walked out before Addison could respond, and Wes silently applauded her technique.

On the way down the hall, they didn't speak, then as they strode through the front door, they met Eric Norcutt coming up the steps toward the office.

"Hey, man," Norcutt said, slapping hands with Wes. "Caught the investigation gig, I heard."

"Yeah. Eric, this is Captain Hughes, the arson investigator. Captain, Eric Norcutt, Baxter PD."

Despite Norcutt's smart-ass comments the other night about women working with the cops, the officer smiled at Cara, probably because he'd gotten a good look at her in daylight and decided she wouldn't be too tough to work with after all. "How's it goin', Captain? Need any help?"

Cara gave Norcutt an impatient, very slight smile. "I've got it handled. Thanks."

So much for the female Columbo routine. The thought almost cheered Wes up. "What are you doing here?" Wes asked Norcutt.

Norcutt nodded at Addison's office building. "Moonlighting. Addison thought he could use extra security at some of his properties."

"Mmm." Clever of the jerk, wasn't it? "We'll let you get to it, then."

"I'm going to Vegas next weekend, Wes. Wanna come?

"Not this time." Really, not ever. He didn't see the appeal.

Norcutt shrugged and pushed open the door. "Nice to meet you, Captain."

She glared after him. "Uh-huh."

As Wes and Cara started toward the truck, another officer slammed the patrol car door, then jogged toward them. He nodded as he passed. "I guess everybody could use an extra buck or two," Wes commented. "So, what did you think?"

"About Addison?"

"Yeah."

"Oh, I liked him."

5

WES'S HAND flinched on the truck's passenger door handle. "You *liked* him?"

"Well, not exactly. *Like's* probably too strong a word. He's just not what I expected." Cara cut her gaze in his direction as she climbed inside. "Probably all those high recommendations from you."

He slammed the door, then rounded the truck, fighting to hold on to his temper with every step. "I can't believe you bought all that crap about wanting to be discreet," he said as he started the engine. "Everybody knows he's slept with half the women in the county. I warned you, remember? Ninety-nine percent—"

"I didn't say I believed him. I just understand the appeal, woman to man."

Wes whipped his head toward her. "You were *attracted* to him?"

"Maybe it's a chemical thing," she said casually, retrieving her pistol and holster from the glove box. "He's pretty to look at. I don't think I'd trust him, but I can certainly see his appeal."

His stomach in knots, he pulled out of the parking lot. "Oh, good. I'd hate to think all those women had lousy taste."

"He's more charming than I expected, though I see what Monica meant. He's used to being the center of attention. I mean, did you see the way the track lighting over his desk highlighted his head?"

Finally, Wes had something to smile about. He and the sharp captain did think a great deal alike. And if she wanted chemistry…he'd damn well show her chemistry. "The center of attention, huh? Kind of like our clever arsonist."

Her brow wrinkled as if she were considering his suggestion carefully. "Could be, though I don't see the slick Mr. Addison getting his hands that dirty."

"You still think we're dealing with a hired gun?"

"Certainly a professional or someone who's done a great deal of research."

"But you're reserving judgment on Addison."

"I'm not eliminating him."

He clenched the steering wheel. What did she *think*, though? "What does your gut say about him? Don't you get one look at a suspect, and instantly think guilty or innocent?"

"No." He sensed her gaze shifting toward him. "Generally, Lieutenant, I listen to what the evidence tells me. Personally, all I thought about Mr. Addison was that he would be a fairly charming dinner companion."

He snorted. "You two certainly seemed to get along well."

"I was playing a part, using an investigative technique, as you well know."

"Well, you're a damn good actress."

She shrugged. "Just playing to an expected stereotype."

"You know he'll check you out, though, and learn you're the state's top arson investigator."

"And figure I slept my way to the top, like everybody else."

A trace of resentment had crept into her voice that she surely hadn't intended to let slip. "I didn't think that," he reminded her quietly.

Out of the corner of his eye, he saw her smile. "Really? You're certainly in the minority."

He said nothing for several moments. They would be at the firehouse in less than five minutes. He might regret the impulse later, but he had to know. He didn't want to examine too closely why. "What about suspects?"

"*What* about suspects?"

He pulled to stop at the traffic light and turned toward her, propping his forearm on the steering wheel. "Do you sleep with suspects?"

Her expressive eyes flashed with anger. "Though I don't see how that's any of your business, no, I don't. We already went over my views on mixing business and pleasure, remember?"

"Addison is certainly a catch. Money, power, influence."

"You have *got* to be kidding." She slipped off her jacket, shrugging into her shoulder holster. "We aren't having this conversation."

"Why the hell not?"

"We work together. It's not appropriate and—"

Wes laughed. "Appropriate? Baby, please—"

"I'm *not* your baby."

Blaahhhh!

The horn blaring behind them forced Wes to

stomp on the gas pedal. He drove a few feet down the road, then pulled over to the side. He bowed his head and kept his hands on the steering wheel, mainly because he wanted to grab her and figured he'd get slugged or shot for his efforts. The idea of Addison and Cara together had him really screwed up, though. How could he and that prick have the same taste in women? Again.

He wanted her, dammit. Addison couldn't have her.

But Cara wasn't his former girlfriend—the one who dumped him for Addison nearly six months ago, starting this compelling itch in his gut that the man was up to no good in more ways than just stealing other guys' dates, this itch that had him digging into Addison's financial status and lack of business ethics. Cara was sharp as a tack, and there was no way she'd fallen for Addison's concerned, victimized citizen act.

His frustration at the moment stemmed from a deep, personal place that Cara had touched the moment he'd laid eyes on her. A sense that he'd found a kindred spirit, someone who might actually feel the same sense of being at odds with the world and lonely because of that.

"What are we going to do about us, Cara?"

"*Us?* There's no us."

Okay. That was it. He'd reached his limit.

He moved quickly, flicking the release on her seat belt and dragging her into his lap before she realized his intention and could do more than lay her hand on the butt of her gun. He cupped the back of her neck. Their faces were less than two inches apart. "Go ahead. Do it. Shoot me. It'd be less painful than watching you and Addison drool all over each other."

Her breathing quickened, and the scent of gardenias enveloped him again. "What's *with* you?"

"You. You're with me." He drew in a breath, then let out the air, part of him so glad to be touching her that he didn't much care if she was pissed. "I can't stop thinking about you."

Her throat moved as she swallowed. "We work together."

"Doesn't matter. I still want you."

"We hardly know each other."

"I know plenty," he said softly, pulling her closer, then pressing his lips against hers. He angled his head and slid his tongue past her lips. She was soft and warm and heavenly. And his. For the moment. Until she came to her senses and realized he was a mistake.

She returned his caress, her hands clutching the front of his shirt, her jeans-clad backside warming his thighs. "This is a mistake," she murmured against his mouth.

"Probably," he said, though he only tightened his grip on her head and deepened their kiss again. He slid his hand between her legs, rubbing along the seam of her jeans, feeling the heat of her body through the thick material.

She moaned in the back of her throat, squirming on his lap, rocking her hips against his hand, silently asking for more. Her tongue glided against his, seducing him into forgetting they were in his truck, in full daylight, parked on the side of the road.

Until another horn blared as a car passed by.

She jerked back, her breath heaving as she stared at him. "I've lost my mind."

He worked up a smile. "So glad it's contagious."

Letting go of his shirt, she scooted back to her side of the truck. "That won't happen again."

"Yes, it will."

She ran her fingers through her hair, obviously trying to smooth the mussed strands. "Look, Lieutenant—"

"My *name*," he ground out. "Use my name."

Angling her body toward him, she drew a bracing breath. "*Wes*, I thought I already explained—I don't get involved with colleagues." As if she sensed his imminent correction, she added, "Or subordinates."

"You can make an exception."

She rubbed her temples. "Why me? You must have dozens of women after you."

He smiled and brushed his thumb across her cheek. "How flattering. Dozens might be a stretch, though."

Her gaze met his, her blue-green eyes, confused and probing, fixed on his. "This is about me interviewing Addison. You really wad yourself up about that man. You were actually, what…jealous?"

"*That* was interviewing? Gee, somehow I missed the hot lights and bamboo shoots under the fingernails."

"Why are you being difficult about this?"

"Because I don't see the problem. I want you. You want me. Let's satisfy each other."

"It's not that simple."

"Yes, it is."

"I need time to think."

"No, you don't. You know what you want. You just don't think you should give in to it."

She scowled. "Have I explained that *your* intuition about *my* feelings is very annoying?"

He pulled away from the curb. "You have till seven tonight to decide."

"Why seven?"

"That's when I'm showing up at your door with wine and Italian food."

"That's very presumptuous."

"Yeah, but you're an intelligent woman. I'm betting by then you can find a way to separate the professional stuff from our personal relationship."

"I really don't like the fact that you're taking control of this."

As he made the turn into the firehouse parking lot, he slid his hand across her thigh. "I know."

He chanced a glance at her, noting she was still scowling, but not quite as hard. Progress? Hell, he hoped so, since the next step was begging.

"Oh, damn," he said as he turned his attention back to his driving.

"See, there's already a problem. I knew when you quit thinking with your—"

"Not with us. With them." He pointed through the windshield at the restless crowd of people at the entrance to the firehouse.

"Well, hell. Reporters."

"YES, WE'RE INVESTIGATING the fires," Cara said into the microphone shoved in her face. "Yes, an as-yet-unidentified man has lost his life. Beyond that, I have no comment."

Only past, long-suffering experience with the relentless Atlanta press kept her moving forward through the throng of reporters. The comforting presence of Wes's hand against her back didn't hurt either.

"Captain Hughes, can you confirm the total loss of two properties owned by prominent local businessman Robert Addison?"

"Yes."

"Are you confirming reports of a serial arsonist loose in Baxter?"

"There have been two seemingly related fires in as many weeks."

"Do you have any suspects?"

"Yes."

"Who?"

She just shook her head to that one, and, as she'd finally reached the doors to the firehouse the reporters had been crowding, she considered having them cited for obstruction of a fire zone. But she decided to humor them for a few minutes. There wasn't much to this case yet, and surely there were bigger fish to fry in metro Atlanta.

"Anyone in custody?" fired off a blond woman who usually handled the north Atlanta suburban beat.

"Not yet."

"But you're confident you'll solve the case?"

"Yes."

Some Ken-doll look-alike pressed his microphone closer, bumping her mouth. "Is it true you've interviewed Robert Addison in regards to these crimes and consider him your prime suspect?"

Cara took a moment to send a warning glare at Ken, shoved the microphone away from her face, then said, "I've interviewed Robert Addison, and I have no prime suspect at this time."

She was halfway through the door Wes held open when Ken's perfect face and his persistent microphone intruded. "But you haven't eliminated him either," the reporter said.

She met Ken's gaze. Maybe these guys could dig up something about Addison, some *proof* of financial stress, that the authorities hadn't. She was likely opening up a PR nightmare for Ben, the mayor, even Wes. But their suspect was paying close attention to the news, and that man she'd found burned to nothing in the ashes gave her license to push back a bit.

"No, I haven't eliminated him," she said to Ken, then slipped through the door as the crowd roared.

"WHAT A DAMN MESS," Ben commented, peeking through the blinds on his office windows.

From across the room, Cara eyed the chief warily. "I probably could have handled the situation better."

He glanced back at her. "You gave them Addison deliberately."

She suppressed the flinch that wanted to escape. "They already had him. I just nudged them."

Ben's gaze darted to his brother, who sat on the edge of his desk. He frowned.

The vein along Wes's jaw throbbed. "I said nothing."

"I know," Ben said, though it seemed he wanted to blame Wes. His gaze slid to Cara. "That's why I brought you in, you know—to keep us all honest."

"I never assumed you were less than honest, Chief," Cara replied.

"But I'm a mayor-appointed official in this town, and the mayor is an elected official—"

"And Robert Addison is an influential resident," she finished.

"I won't let his influence stand in the way of justice," Ben said.

Cara leaned back in her chair and smiled cynically. "But it would be nice to blame the whole fiasco on an outsider—should it come to that."

"No, I—"

"None of this is Cara's fault, Ben," Wes said, standing, his fists clenched, his body angled toward his brother. "Those reporters were blocking the door of the damn firehouse. I'd have arrested them if she'd let me. You won't blame *anything* on her."

Ben's eyebrows disappeared into his hairline. His gaze bounced from Wes to Cara and back.

Cara forced her face to sober. She didn't know Ben Kimball that well, and since she was giving him a hard time, he might decide to return the favor.

She hadn't risked professional respect for a temporary roll in the hay yet, but Wes was approaching irresistible status. No, she *could* resist him. She just didn't *want* to.

And she really loved Italian food.

"It's a risk I take, Lieutenant," she said quietly, hoping Wes would get the hint and downshift. Oh, yeah, *sure* they could separate the professional stuff from the personal. As flattered as part of her wanted to be by his defense, she knew it would ultimately only complicate the case further. If that was possible.

But Wes either didn't get the hint, or didn't care. "You don't understand how these people work, Cara," he said, still glaring at Ben. "Mayor Collins and my dear brother here play strictly by the rules.

He probably wouldn't *approve* of our little visit to Addison today."

"On the contrary, *little* brother," Ben began, his eyes as hard and cold as diamonds, "I received great compliments from Mr. Addison about the captain's visit." His gaze darted briefly to Cara. "Though I got the distinct impression he was more interested in her body than her investigative prowess."

"Sounds just like him. I've been telling you and the mayor for months that Addison's communications system 'gift' wasn't as generous as it seemed. He's going to pressure us to drop this."

"Dammit, Wes, you don't know that."

A muscle pulsed along Wes's jaw. "Yes, I do."

Though her chest tightened, Cara examined her fingernails as if they were the most interesting thing in the world. There was a victim in this case, but, like so many others, he wasn't a priority. "You know, I'd fire a warning shot into the ceiling, but I'd rather not get a bill from the mayor."

The brothers continued to glare at each other for several long moments, during which Cara prayed they'd either relax or punch each other and get it over with. In a way, she wanted to help foster peace, but she knew her presence was only going to make matters worse. She tried to focus on what was actually relevant to her case.

"Guys, we're doing this strictly by-the-book—carefully, even diplomatically." She shrugged. "At least until that option is no longer viable. Robert Addison is a suspect—I'd even venture to say a really good suspect, though I'd deny that to the press—but we still have lots of evidence to sort through, witnesses and suspects to question. This case isn't going to be pretty or easy for anybody, but that's not something we can control." She rose casually from her chair, leaning against Ben's desk as the brothers continued to stare at each other, though they had, at least, backed up a step from all-out slugging. "I don't really much care who I piss off around here. I sympathize with you, Ben, that you have to live with the aftermath. And I don't want to make an already tense situation worse for Wes, but I gotta tell you…I'm not here for either one of you. Not anymore."

Finally, they turned toward her.

And she let loose the full force of her anger.

"In most arson cases, unless you watched the perp toss the match into the building, you'll never get him. Hell, these days you can't just have watched him. You'd better damn well have it on videotape. *Intent to set* is the best you'll get. Insurance fraud—maybe. Even the death of that poor man isn't murder. When we get this guy, he'll be charged with manslaughter—max. Kill a firefighter, and you get murder, but that's only because it's a federal crime."

Wes took a step toward her. "Cara, we didn't mean—"

"The only reason this case is so high priority," she continued, her heart picking up even more speed, "is because a prominent businessman is out two warehouses. But I want justice for that poor man we found in the ashes. The one nobody cares about, the one who'll be forgotten come spring…."

She drew a deep breath. She'd gotten too caught up in the details—again. Not every case had to be a replay of her parents' deaths. That bastard had been convicted and died in prison long ago. Not every perp was *him*. Not every case revolved around her pain.

Yet, no matter how many times she told herself those facts, the past never seemed to go away.

"Get her some water," Wes said, his hand on her arm.

She shrugged him off. "I'm fine. I don't need anything." *Or anyone.* She walked toward the windows, though she didn't peek through the blinds as Ben had done. She knew what she'd find on the other side. Reality. Chaos.

Sometimes she really needed a bit of peace.

Wes appeared next to her, a cup of water extended in his hand. "Drink it."

She did, but only because she figured she'd already caused enough problems. As the silence lengthened, she could feel both men's stares. Crushing the empty paper cup in her fist, she pushed the past back into its dark closet and lifted her chin. "Sorry. I was out of line."

Ben shook his head, then glanced at his brother. "I didn't see anything out of line. What about you, Wes?"

Wes shrugged. "We were talking about the case, I thought."

Cara exchanged a long, silent look with Wes, then breathed a mental sigh of relief. If the brothers had coddled her or sympathized, she'd have been humiliated. Nearly all her life people had looked at her differently, had considered her an outsider, her ideas and goals strange. How was it she'd suddenly discovered so many who simply took her for who she was?

"Right. The case." She rolled her shoulders. "I think we should watch Addison very closely. If he is our guy—by his own hand or by hire—he should be watched just on principle. If he's not, then our perp certainly has him in mind as a target…eventually, anyway."

Ben angled his head. "You think the arsonist will go after Addison directly?"

"Oh, yeah. If the arsonist is targeting Addison's properties, the fires are incidental, a way to hurt Addison where he lives."

"His pocketbook," Wes put in.

"Right. Addison has insurance, of course, so the money doesn't mean much. But it's the inconvenience, the constant fear of when the next disaster will occur that fuels the arsonist. With the ultimate goal being elimination of the object of his hatred."

The corners of Wes's mouth turned up. "Maybe we shouldn't be so quick to solve this one."

Ben nudged his brother. "Your grudge doesn't go so far that you'd want him dead."

For some reason, Wes stared at Cara as he answered. "No, it doesn't."

"So," Ben said, crossing the room to sit behind his desk. "We're back to interviews and evidence-gathering."

"It's not fun or sexy," Cara said, "but that's where we'll find him. No matter how clever the perp, no matter how careful, mistakes are always made."

Looking stern, Wes crossed his arms over his chest. "And neither snow, nor sleet—"

"Nor dark of night, blah, blah, blah," she finished for him. She walked toward Ben. "I haven't had too many get away from me yet. I don't expect to start now."

Again, Ben's gaze flicked from her to his brother. "I'm sure you haven't."

Being an astute guy, the chief had obviously sensed the sparks between her and Wes. The very idea caused a nervous flutter in her belly. She didn't need more complication. *I still want you,* Wes had said earlier. No denying that. How much should she risk to give into that want? Or was she really risking anything at all professionally? Was it just her own internal defenses she didn't want to compromise?

She didn't have time to explore that idea, since a tap on the office door interrupted her train of thought.

"Come in," Ben called.

"Unless you're from the press," Wes added as he sank into a chair in front of his brother's desk.

The intruders weren't from the press, but still just as invasive. Skyler and Monica stood at the entrance. All smiles, they walked—in Monica's case, she slinked—inside, and the men immediately jumped to their feet. Monica and her husband cooed and smooched with each other, while Skyler scowled at Wes as if he'd purposefully missed the annual family reunion.

Finally, everybody turned their attention to her. Since that was a place Cara wasn't comfortable in the least, she edged toward the door. "Well, I've got evidence to sort through, reports to file, so I'll just be on my way."

"Oh, no!" the other women exclaimed at the same time.

"We actually came here to see you," Skyler said.

Monica's sharp gaze met Cara's. "We're here to rescue you."

"Rescue me from what?" Cara looked from the girls to the guys. Truthfully, she was much happier discussing motives, fire codes, investigative procedures and autopsy reports. "I've got a case to solve."

Monica and Skyler charged toward her, each grabbing an arm. "But it's after five. You've been working all day. You need a break."

Cara wanted to dig in her heels, but she was so surprised by the ambush she didn't have a chance. Instead, she swallowed her fear. "I'm fine. Really."

Skyler's big, supposedly innocent blue eyes widened. "You're fine. Really?"

Monica—hip out in a provocative pose—opened the door. "But when we're through with you, you'll be better than fine."

"Yeah, but—"

Cara never had to opportunity to finish her protest. The last sight she had was of Ben's grin and Wes's scowl.

6

"OKAY, BUT CAN I just say..." Cara stared into the dwindling bottom of her watermelon martini. "You chicks scare me."

Monica laughed. Skyler pursed her lips.

To add to the troubling idea of being forced into a girls' night out, Cara had quickly realized that the other two girls weren't of the same mind. Monica seemed to think the idea of her hooking up with Wes was the greatest connection since the Internet. Skyler, however, had obviously reconsidered her matchmaking ideas.

How these two had figured out she and Wes had been making eyes at each other, Cara had no idea. Frankly, her colleagues—even the governor—had consistently complimented her on her ability to play both sides, to be neutral, to be aggressive, to hide her feelings, to...well, be an actor should this whole arson investigator thing not work out.

"And Wes and I aren't sleeping together," she added, just to be sure they were all clear.

Monica smiled. Skyler spewed chardonnay in an arc across the table.

Still smiling, Monica leaned forward. "But for how long?"

Cara had no definitive answer to that, so she just swallowed.

Skyler patted her lips with her napkin. "I think that's for the best. I've been thinking a lot about this since I saw them together this morning. They're too much alike. And Cara's only going to be here for a short time. Wes is tied to this town and his family."

Okay, that'd be a yes for Monica, and a no for Skyler.

Monica sighed. "But who else in this town is going to put up with Wes? He's temperamental, opinionated and moody. Cara is all those things, too." The sexy redhead smiled. "But with a woman's sensibility."

Cara raised a finger. "I—"

"You know I think you're great, Cara," Skyler said. "But you and Wes work in the same field." She turned to Monica. "How hard will it be for him to come home, ready to let the stress of the day fade away, when his partner is just as hyped up about her case as he is about his?" She shook her head. "Bad emotional karma there."

"Who else is going to talk about that stuff with him?" Monica asked.

"His colleagues. He should leave that stuff at the office." Skyler twirled the stem of her wineglass. "You need peace in the home. How else—"

Skyler stopped as her sister-in-law started laughing. "*Peace?* Like you and Jack have?" Monica waved her well-manicured hand. "Please. You question him about every aspect of his work." At Skyler's scowl, she added, "As well you should. You're partners. Just as Ben and I are. Just because your professional lives don't diverge doesn't mean you can't make your personal life work."

"Aha!" Skyler gestured with her glass. "You see. Our professional lives are opposite to our husbands'. In Cara and Wes's case, their professional *and* personal lives would be the same."

Since neither woman acted as though she existed, Cara just sipped her drink. Would alcohol lead to insight about her case? Would she finally understand the tension between Wes and Ben? The rivalry between Wes and Addison?

She doubted it.

She glanced around the busy sports bar. The decor was simple—black vinyl booths lined the walls in a U-shape, tables scattered in the center. The long oak bar catered to a dozen or so beer-drinking patrons, several of whom she recognized from both the firehouse and the police station. None were in uniform, however. She suspected Ben's professionalism and the mayor's itchy political conscience had contributed to the policy of no drinking in uniform, even off duty.

She tuned back in to the conversation/argument between Monica and Skyler, only to catch the phrases "time to settle down" and "...about kids."

"Helloooo?" Cara waved her hand in front of the women's faces. "I'm hot for the man. That doesn't mean I want to get a mortgage, a membership in the PTO and settle into a life of Mayor Collins-driven politics."

"Aha!" Monica said.

"What's wrong with having a mortgage?" Skyler asked, indignant.

Hoping they would just go away, Cara gulped her martini. She wasn't much of a drinker, but the thing wasn't bad—kind of like a potent Jolly Rancher. And nearly at the bottom of the glass, her tongue was numb anyway.

"I *knew* you were hot for him," Monica said, gesturing with her own martini glass. "There's no taking it back now."

Confused, Cara glanced across the table. "Why would I take it back?"

"To keep us from setting the two of you up. Now there's no excuse."

Skyler raised her finger. "Excuse me, *I* don't want to set them up."

"There are plenty of excuses," Cara said, making careful note of Skyler's support in this. "One, we work together. Two, I don't get involved with colleagues. Three, I need to concentrate on this case. Four, I don't sleep with everybody I'm 'hot for.' Five and six belong to Skyler—we're too much alike, and we're only temporarily in proximity to each other."

Scowling, Monica tapped her long nails—painted turquoise and white to match her pantsuit—against the table. "You don't ever do anything just for the hell of it?"

"No."

"You've never been involved with a colleague?"

"No."

"Never been tempted?"

"No."

"You don't, like, get…urges?"

Cara met those perceptive green eyes head-on. *No way around that one.* "Yes."

"Ah—"

"Not uncontrollable urges, though."

Instead of arguing, which Cara could have handled easily, Monica smiled and shrugged. "Then you're missing out, aren't you?"

No matter how hard she fought it, Cara saw the image of her and Wes outside her apartment, a hungry look on his face as his head descended toward hers. The way he'd lost control that afternoon and dragged her into his lap. The way he slid his hand between her legs, gliding his thumb against the seam of her jeans.

Her stomach contracted, then released.

Okay, maybe I was a little hasty about that uncontrollable thing….

As if Monica sensed capitulation, her smile widened.

"I'm not sure about this…" Skyler began, her gaze darting from Monica to Cara. "What about the case? We need this nut caught. *Our* husbands are fighting those fires, remember? And what about them being so alike? The fact that they're geographically incompatible?"

Monica rolled her eyes, as if annoyed she had to prove her point further. "Geography can be adjusted. As for the other… " Again, her gaze met Cara's, and for the first time in a long time—at least since the last time she saw Wes—Cara resisted the urge to squirm. "Why are you so successful at investigating?"

"I never give up, and my bullshit meter is set to extrasensitive."

"See," Monica said to Skyler, "she'll solve the case regardless of her relationship with Wes. They're perfect for each other."

"Good evening, ladies," a male voice said smoothly.

Cara glanced up at the gorgeous, black-haired,

blue-eyed man who'd stopped at their table. The last time she'd seen him he'd been sweaty, sooty and in full turn-out gear. Damn, he packed quite a punch when he cleaned up.

"Steven, what perfect timing," Skyler said, her eyes lighting. "Cara, this is my other brother—the baby—Steven. He's a firefighter, too."

Baby Kimball aimed his twinkling gaze and smile at Cara. "Since I turned twelve, most people have called me Steve. And we already met the other night, right, Captain Hughes?"

Maybe it was just her suspicion of nearly everyone, of charming men in particular—especially after her encounter with Addison—but Steven "call me Steve" Kimball had her narrowing her eyes. "Right."

"I've heard a lot about you," Steve said, sliding his way into Cara's side of the booth. "An understatement, I guess, given the spotlight of this arson case."

Smooth didn't even begin to describe Steve Kimball. The Southern charm was there, of course, but his accent was ambivalent, as if he'd spent a lot of time away from his heritage. And he didn't seem to fall in line with either his taciturn fire chief brother, or Wes's barely controlled rebelliousness.

Seeming to sense all this, Skyler said, "Steven was an exchange student in Italy during high school, then he went away to university in London and France, before coming back home to Baxter."

Cara lifted her eyebrows. "To fulfill your dream of being a firefighter in a one-firehouse town?"

He simply smiled. "Something like that."

Cara shrugged and glanced at her watch. Six forty-five. Did she stay and hang out, thereby standing up

Wes and possibly pissing him off to the point that he'd give up on her? Or did she lighten up and find out whether uncontrollable urges were something she'd been missing out on?

Her body and her brain were at war, and she found herself exploring emotions within herself that she didn't acknowledge very often. The need for companionship. The longing for satisfaction. The desire to have a man look at her as if no other woman existed.

"You're not what I expected," Steve said, leaning closer to her, his forearms on the table.

Noting his proximity with irritation, Cara deliberately took her time examining him from head to hip—all that she could see above the table.

He was about as close to physically perfect as any man she'd ever seen, but then, perfection made her itchy. She much preferred the slight bump on Wes's nose, which he'd no doubt broken at some point. The close-cropped goatee on Wes's face that made him look just a bit too wild and dangerous. The irritated scowl he didn't bother to hide most of the time.

By contrast, Baby Steven looked as if he spent more time at the salon than Monica and oozed charm as easily as most people breathed.

She returned her gaze to his. "And you were expecting…"

"Someone tougher."

Cara nearly choked. "Pardon me?"

He smiled. "For a gun-toting, boot-wearing, knife-under-the-pillow lady, you're really quite lovely."

"I don't sleep with a knife under my pillow." *I keep a switchblade in my boot.* "Some idiotic reporter made that up."

"But you do carry a gun?"

"Usually."

"Why?"

"So I can shoot the bad guys."

Steve angled his head. "Fascinating."

Monica cleared her throat loudly. "Hey, loverboy, this one's taken."

Steve's gaze dropped to Cara's hands. "I don't think so."

"By Wes," Monica added.

Steve's eyes widened briefly. "Oh, yeah?"

"Yes," Monica said.

"I'm not so sure," Skyler said at the same time.

This is ridiculous.

"Hop up, Baby Steven," she said to her flirty boothmate. "I've gotta go."

"Don't go," Monica said, grabbing Cara's hand. "We won't bug you anymore about Wes. Promise." She glanced at her sister-in-law. "Right, Sky?"

"*Me?* This was all *your* idea. I don't think—"

"We're just worried about you," Monica said, slicing a *be quiet* look at Skyler. "You're lonely."

Feeling her face heat, Cara darted a look at Steve, who was now standing beside the table, certainly intrigued by this whole exchange.

Great. Try to act cool, and your *friends* blow your image with a word.

"I'll see you guys later," she said as she scooted out of the booth. Thank God she'd insisted on bringing her own car. "Thanks for the drink."

"This is all my fault," Skyler said. "I've insulted you. I just—" She glanced at Monica, then rushed on, "The last time I thought I'd found a woman for Wes it worked out rather badly, so..."

"You didn't insult me," Cara said, touched by Skyler's concern for her feelings. She'd had exactly three conversations with her—including this one—yet she felt as though she'd known her for years. She'd taken the bantering disagreement between them about Wes as an out-loud discussion of actions and consequences. Cara did that silently with herself all the time on a case. It was always good to hear the pros and cons laid out, and she found herself glad to have new friends to share problems with—even if the whole business had begun with their insistence and her reluctance.

That she was discussing something so personal with women—and a man—she'd met only recently showed the ability of the Kimballs to get under your skin. They drew you into their fold so quickly you barely realized how you'd gotten there.

"I appreciate everybody's opinions," she said to Skyler. "You guys were really great to include me."

Skyler looked relieved, and Cara felt slightly odd, but good.

She nodded at Steve. "Nice to see you again."

He smiled. "You might want to consider keeping your gun unloaded around Wes."

"Yeah?"

His eyes danced. "He's been known to drive women to extreme action."

Skyler glared at him.

Monica pushed Steven into the booth. "Shut up."

Cara shook her head at the threesome as she walked away. She had the feeling she needed to do further investigating in the matter of Wes Kimball.

His family seemed just as concerned about her as they did him. How would it really feel to be part of a unit like that? Warm and comfortable? Or overwhelming?

Though no family was perfect. There was clearly tension between Wes and Ben. Opposing personalities? Definitely. But there seemed to be more. Wes clearly respected his older brother, yet he resented him at the same time. Because Ben was higher ranked? Somehow that didn't seem likely, given his annoyance with the mayor's posturing.

The family dynamic seemed to center around Ben as the patriarch, so she could certainly see Wes chaffing under his conservative rule. But then—

Was any of that even her business? She wanted to sleep with the man, not analyze his family relationships.

Skyler and Monica had definitely helped on that score. She and Wes were attracted to each other. They were going to be forced to spend a lot of time together in the next few weeks. They were so similar compatibility wasn't an issue. But long-term didn't seem a good idea for either of them.

She stepped outside into the muggy night. Fall was here one minute, then retreating like a scared cat the next. She slid off her leather jacket as she climbed into her government-issue white sedan.

Then, for good measure, she locked her pistol in the glove compartment.

She hoped he brought veal parmesan.

SHIFTING HIS LOAD of lasagna, veal parmesan, salad, garlic bread and Chianti, Wes checked his watch again. Seven-twenty. Had she left or was she deliberately staying away?

Neither idea boded well for his night of romance.

He'd thought the direct approach would be best with Cara, but maybe not. He could have asked Steve for advice, but he didn't really think his brother's suave moves would work for him. He'd just feel like an idiot.

Oh, kind of like you do right now?

Sighing, he set down his sack of groceries, then searched his pockets for his cell phone. No point standing around and torturing himself all night.

He had her cell number half-dialed when he heard someone approaching. Turning, he watched her climb the last few steps and walk toward him.

His heart jumped into high gear. His breathing grew labored.

And suddenly he didn't feel so stupid. She was within his grasp. He'd finally find out what went on inside that busy brain of hers, how her skin felt beneath her tough exterior.

His gaze roved her face as she drew closer. Still wearing the same jeans and white shirt she'd had on all day, he noted her leather jacket, pistol and holster were missing. Unarmed was good. But she wasn't smiling, or looking particularly welcoming.

Then again, maybe she'd shove him off her doorstep and tell him to get lost.

He picked up the bag. "Hi."

She stopped next to him and unlocked her apartment door. The scent of gardenias washed over him, and he fought to breathe through his mouth. Losing the little bit of control he had left wouldn't help. "Hi," she said.

"Have you eaten?"

Her gaze met his, giving away none of her feelings. "No."

"Want to?"

She shrugged. "Sure."

She preceded him inside, and he followed. At least he'd made it past the door. And he hadn't even resorted to begging. Yet.

Her apartment was plain, obviously outfitted with rental furniture and accessories. She hadn't set out any pictures or knickknacks. Beige walls, beige carpet, a picture of mountains on the wall above the taupe sofa, a small dinette in the far corner, an almond-colored Formica bar separating the kitchen from the living area. The only evidence of her was a laptop and printer set up on the coffee table.

He strolled toward the kitchen, setting his bag on the counter. Need for her itched along his skin, but he concentrated on keeping his breathing even and holding his urges in check. He wasn't a damn animal. They'd have a nice dinner, some nonwork-related conversation—though what they'd talk about he had no idea—maybe watch a movie on TV. Like a real date. No pressure.

"You got any wineglasses?" he asked, opening the cabinet doors beside the fridge.

"I have no idea."

He'd opened another set of cabinets and spied some goblet-shaped glasses on the top shelf when she spoke from behind him. "I'm not interested in a one-night stand."

Oh, yeah. The direct approach had been best.

Setting the glasses on the counter, he turned. Barefoot, she was standing in the doorway of the kitchen, leaning one shoulder against the frame, her striking aqua eyes focused on his.

"Me either," he said. One night wouldn't be near long enough.

"I'm not interested in forever either."

"I can live with that." He wanted to smile, find a way to tease her. The lady did like her rules and boundaries. But his heart was beating too fast, his erection throbbing too intensely to think straight. "How about the duration of the case?"

She stalked toward him. "Deal," she whispered, then grabbed the front of his shirt and yanked him toward her.

He thrust his arms around her, molding the length of her body against his, even as he angled his head and captured her lips. Hell, who was he kidding? Even breathing? Holding his urges in check?

He'd be lucky if his heart didn't explode.

Deepening their kiss, he slid his hands down her back, cupping her bottom, pressing her against his erection. The pressure of her body against his sent a ripple of pleasure down his spine. He wished he could spend the next several years just exploring her mouth, the curves of her body, anticipating the moment he could glide his hands across her silky skin, but desire was clawing at him, demanding release, urging him to toss civility and finesse.

She moaned deep in her throat, seeming to encourage the intensity his body craved.

He spun them so she was positioned between the countertop and him, then he tugged her shirt from her jeans, stripping the white material over her head in one swift motion. He allowed his gaze a brief sweep of her creamy skin, the swell of her breasts above her nude-colored bra…the stomach muscles that rippled to her waist.

"Damn, woman, work out much?"

She slid her hand through the hair at the back of his head, kissing his lips, then his jaw, then the base of his throat, as her other hand worked the buttons on his shirt. "Exercise releases tension."

He sucked in a breath as she tugged his shirt off his shoulders, flinging it to the floor. "No kidding?"

She rubbed her palms along his sides, then swept back up his chest. "This is more fun, though."

He unhooked the front clasp of her bra, then cupped her breasts. "I agree completely."

Closing her eyes, she dropped her head back. Pleasure danced across her face. Fascinated, Wes smiled and drew his thumbs across her nipples. She gasped, clutching his forearms.

Her silky skin, which he felt as if he'd waited forever to touch, warmed beneath his thumbs and flushed darker with each stroke. When he replaced his hands with his mouth, she trembled. Her nipples hardened to peaks, which he took great pleasure sucking into his mouth.

All the while, he throbbed and ached for her touch.

Drawing his tongue up her chest, then along the side of her neck, he ground his hips against hers. She pushed back, her head lifting, her desire-filled gaze meeting his briefly as her hands dropped to the waistband of his jeans. Dispensing with the buttons in seconds, she slid her hand down his stomach, beneath his underwear—no pausing, no nervous fumbling—straight to his hardness.

He jolted when she wrapped her hand around him, stroking him to teeth-gritting ecstasy. He closed his eyes. He gripped the counter.

"Mmm. Taking control has its advantages," she said.

He forced his eyes open so he could look at her. She somehow managed to smile and still look hungry for more. He remembered their conversation that afternoon in his truck, when she'd said she didn't like him taking control.

If this was her idea of retaliation, bring it on.

She wrapped her other hand around his neck, bringing him close for a kiss. Her breathing labored, she moved her mouth across his, as she continued to stroke his erection. Up, then a brisk slide down, her fingernails catching him beneath the hood.

He suppressed the urge to explode. God, the woman drove him crazy.

"Protection?" she gasped against his lips.

"Back pocket," he mumbled, still desperate to catch his breath.

She slid her hand down his backside, giving him an unexpected jolt of pleasure. She ripped open the package with her teeth, then rolled the condom down the hard length of him.

As if his hormones had suddenly started flashing *now, now* in neon lights, he flipped open the buttons on her jeans, then helped her shove them and her panties down her hips. After she kicked off her clothes, she braced her hands on his forearms as he lifted her onto the counter.

Okay, so the kitchen counter wasn't the most romantic of settings, but it had the advantage of being close, and…being close.

His erection nudged the entrance to her body. She drew a deep breath as she wrapped her legs around him. He kissed her briefly, then pushed inside.

The sensation of becoming part of her hit him immediately. He felt surrounded by her, cradled, needed. Not alone.

As he retreated with his hips, he pulled her head against him, so she was wedged between his neck and shoulder. He surged inside her again, deeper, closer, absorbing every breath, moan and heartbeat.

Struggling with the need to erupt, he tried to set an even pace, but she felt so wonderful, so warm and tight, his control was falling away as if he'd jumped from an airplane. He wasn't sure how much longer he could last. Desperate, he increased his rhythm and the angle of his entry, hoping she'd rush to her peak as quickly as he was.

Her breathing hitched, then she let a long, satisfied moan escape.

He held tight and followed her into ecstasy.

CARA SLID her mouth across Wes's bare shoulder.

Still trying to catch his breath, he groaned. "I need to exercise more if I'm gonna hang out with you."

"I let you lie down, didn't I?"

"I'm not sure. I can't feel my legs."

Smiling, she kissed his lips lightly.

His eyes finally opened, the intensity of his gaze replaced by blurred satisfaction. "Where am I?"

"My bed."

"How did I get here?"

She sat up, bracing her hands against his chest. The light sprinkling of black hairs tickled her palms. She wasn't quite sure what she was doing with him—besides the obvious physical pleasure. When Baxter was nothing but a dot in her rearview mirror, she'd no doubt regret taking this step of intimacy. Something told her Wes Kimball wouldn't be quite as easy to put behind her as other men in her life had been.

But she shook aside looming consequences for the moment. "Turn over, you big baby."

He eyed her warily.

"I'm just going to rub your back."

Grinning, he rolled over, turning his head to one side and folding his arms above his head. Cara, however, was unprepared for the enticing sight of his tanned, muscular, bare back. Her stomach rolled, spreading warmth throughout her body. There was just so darn much of him she didn't know exactly where to begin. With a shrug, she straddled his hips.

"Oh, God," he said.

As she was still naked, with her femininity now resting comfortably at the small of his back, she took that comment as a compliment. She laid the heels of her palms on either side of his spine, then pressed, sliding her hands from his lower back all the way to his neck, repeating the motion several times. Then she used the pads of her fingers to make circular motions across his shoulder blades, down his back. She saved his shoulders for last, squeezing the muscles in her hands, using her thumbs to press along his neck.

Then she started the entire process over again.

She fell into an easy rhythm and quickly became aware of the sensuality of exploring his body, of the spicy, masculine scent clinging to him, of the warmth and smoothness of his skin, of the compactness of his muscles. He was quite fascinating. And she liked having his eyes closed, his back turned, so she could indulge her need to touch him unobserved. When his sharp blue eyes were focused on her, she couldn't think half the time. When he was touching her, she couldn't breathe.

She was so intent on her task, she squeaked in surprise when he grabbed her wrist and pulled her off his back. She found herself lying on her side next to him, his hand resting on her hip.

His gaze captured hers. "You're very good at that."

"Really?" She drew a deep breath and tried to gather her thoughts. "I've never done it before."

He smiled. "I'm your first?"

"Massage victim, yes." Was he going to ask about her past lovers? There wasn't a lot to detail, actually. She'd bet his experience had been different, certainly more plentiful. And she wasn't thrilled to find herself wondering just a little too intently how much those women had meant to him.

Man, sex screwed with more than your body, it messed with your head.

She slid her arms around his neck. "You were so still I thought you'd gone to sleep."

"With you, naked, on my back?" He pulled her

hips against his body, his erection caught between them. "I don't think so."

She smiled. "I think you've recovered."

"Definitely." He rolled her onto her back. Looming over her, he slid his hand along her side, then between their bodies. His fingers glided into the moist heat at the apex of her thighs.

She sucked in a breath and closed her eyes. Nothing legal should feel that good.

He continued moving his fingers up, then down, his thumb pressing the button that had her hunger soaring. Her femininity felt heavy. Her muscles tightened, straining for more…or maybe less. The sensations he invoked were so intense, she thrashed her head against the pillow and clutched the sheets, praying the next move would finally break the tension.

But, somehow, he heightened the pleasure. Her stomach muscles clenched. Her breathing grew ragged. He slid his fingers inside her, his thumb stroking her folds, the nub of her clitoris. She felt suspended on the edge of rapture.

She arched her back. "Please, Wes."

"I like the sound of that," he said in her ear, his breath sending pleasurable chills across her skin. "Please…what?"

"Please…make…it—"

He flicked his thumb over her one last time, and she exploded.

Waves of release crested, fell, then rose again. Each pulse seemed stronger, yet the relief from the gnawing ache rippled down her spine and legs. Her hips bucked, grinding against his hand.

When she finally floated back to her senses, she

found herself staring up at him. The need etched on his face surprised her. With her index finger, she traced the edge of his mustache. "Wes…"

"I'm with you, babe." After snagging a foil packet from the bedside table, he swiftly rolled on the protection, then braced himself on his forearms and slid inside her.

Nerve endings she thought they'd sated jumped back to life. Her heart hammered against her ribs. As she rolled her hips up to meet his, a dart of pleasure shot through her body. Why in the world had she ever questioned the idea of how powerful they'd be together?

She gripped his shoulders as he retreated, pulling his erection halfway out, then drove himself back inside. Tingles blossomed out from the center of her body, igniting her blood, and a wild craving for satisfaction twisted her muscles.

Wrapping her legs around his hips, she groaned at the deeper penetration of his thrusts. Sweat beaded on her forehead, slid down her back. She closed her eyes, absorbing the intensity of the sensations, the wild pounding of her pulse.

Her orgasm hovered just on the horizon one second, then slammed into her the next. Her hips came off the bed. Her heart rate shot skyward. And even as she shivered with pleasure, he drove himself into her one last time, his body finally joining hers in completion.

7

CARA STRETCHED her arms above her head. "I'm hungry."

"I wonder why," Wes muttered, his face buried in the pillow. He turned his head, and they found themselves almost nose to nose. An unmistakable look of affection and tenderness passed through his eyes.

Should she say something about how she felt? Whatever that was. Should she compliment him? Tease him?

The moment passed, and he rolled off the bed, glancing around. "I have pants somewhere."

Groggy and confused, Cara sat up, then slid to the edge of the bed. "In the kitchen, I think."

He laid his hands on her shoulders. "How about I heat everything up and bring it in here?"

"Eat in *bed?*"

"Sure." He kissed her forehead, then turned, walking toward the door.

She tilted her head sideways to watch him stride, bare-assed, from the room. How in the world was she going to concentrate on arson evidence and questioning suspects, knowing all *that* was under his clothes?

Shaking aside the image, she forced her body to

move toward the bathroom. She hopped in the shower, reveling in the spray of hot, streaming water over her skin. Afterwards, as she slid into her robe, she decided the jury needed further deliberation on the subject of uncontrollable urges. She couldn't deny sex was a necessary tension reliever, a reminder not to take life so seriously, and—when one was doing it with Wes Kimball—the most pleasurable way on earth to exercise. But her stomach felt all squishy, and her heart contracted whenever she looked into his eyes. The moments their bodies had been connected, she'd felt as if every part of her—heart and soul—were also part of him.

The intimacy was emotional, as well as physical. And she wasn't sure if that was a good thing.

She was here temporarily. Her career was her main focus in her life. They both liked to control things. They both had strong opinions. They'd even laid out a time limit for this relationship.

As she opened the bathroom door, she considered deeper ramifications. What if she embarrassed herself or the state arson department, or—worse—lost her focus on this case and someone else lost their life....

The low, smooth sounds of Toni Braxton's unique R&B voice wound their way into the room. He'd found her CD player.

"I like your taste in music," Wes said as he appeared in the doorway.

He'd put on his jeans and nothing else. She swallowed hard. She'd practically attacked the man twice. She really needed to find some restraint where he was concerned.

She clenched her hands together behind her. "Thanks."

He turned, extending his hand to the bed behind him. "How about some dinner?"

Glancing past him, she noticed he'd pulled the comforter over the sheets and laid steaming plates of food, utensils and salad bowls on the bed. The smell of cheese and rich tomato sauce had her nearly falling to her knees. "Yum."

He snaked his arm around her waist, pulling her against his body. "Is that for me or the food?"

She glanced up at him. Again, she had to fight for her breath as his gaze met hers. "Both." Then, striving for a light tone, she shoved his shoulder. "Now, out of my way. I think I smell veal parmesan."

Chuckling, he stepped aside as she made a beeline for the bed. "You do."

She plopped on the mattress and dove in, groaning with undiluted pleasure when the spicy, herb-infused sauce hit her tongue. "Where in Baxter did you find *this?*"

"If you know where to look…"

"You're not going to tell me."

"Nope," he said as he forked up a bite of lasagna. "You'll have to come to me for your Italian fix."

During dinner, they talked about everything but the case that had brought them together. On the subject of sports she preferred NASCAR; he liked college football. Favorite TV shows? He liked gritty crime dramas; she preferred sitcoms. Vacation spots? They both agreed on anywhere warm and beachy. Local politics? They agreed Mayor Collins was two rhinestones short of a full necklace.

She somehow wound up with a half-full glass of Chianti in her hand and her head in his lap as he reclined against her headboard.

He twirled a strand of her hair around his finger. "You said earlier you'd never given a massage to anyone. A comment like that will boost a man's ego."

"I've had other lovers of course."

"But none as good as me."

That assessment was way too true to acknowledge seriously. She rolled her eyes. "Naturally." She lifted her head and sipped from her wineglass. "Actually, the last man I gave a massage to was my dad."

He coughed. "Your dad?"

"Yeah." She felt her face heat. She hadn't intended for that admission to slide out. But now, she couldn't stop the flow of memories. Her dad coming home from a hard day at the textile mill, his muscles exhausted, his body aching. She'd order him to lie on the floor, then she'd take off her shoes and walk across his back.

But, as always, the brief glimpse of hominess was replaced by the pain that came later. The emptiness she was sure she'd never fill.

"You still close to him?" he asked.

"No. He's dead."

Wes's body tensed. "What happened?"

She pressed her lips together. They said it would get easier to admit. When, exactly, did that happen? "He was killed in a fire. My mother, too."

His hand gripped hers. "Both of them? How old were you?"

"Ten."

"What happened to you afterward?"

From long practice, she fought back her emotions. "Orphanage."

He stroked his thumb back and forth across her wrist. As she glanced up at him, she noted he was staring at the wall. Was he even aware of his actions? Probably not, but his touch comforted her anyway. "Is that why you became an arson investigator?" he asked.

"Yes."

He was silent for a moment, then he said, "That's why you were so concerned about the homeless guy. Did no one take interest in your parents' case?"

"Not until a congressman's daughter and her boyfriend wound up as victims of the same guy." She had to pause and swallow. "He was convicted of serial arson and multiple homicide. He died in prison several years ago."

Wes sat perfectly still for a moment, then he laid their joined hands on her stomach. He dipped his head. "My dad was killed in a fire, too."

She clenched her hand around her glass. The kinship hadn't been lost on her when Ben had suggested Wes as a liaison. "I heard."

"The other night...did you...did it all come back?"

"Yes."

"Does it always?"

"Yes." She closed her eyes, then forced them open again. "It's not something you get past, really. It's a part of you that you simply have to deal with. Sometimes it helps. It reminds you who the real victims are. But pain and memories will always motivate you." She paused, and when he didn't comment, she added, "You can't pretend you don't know what I mean."

Saying nothing, he sighed.

Cara could imagine the thoughts going through his mind. Would it ever end? Would peace ever come? And the worst—*why me?*

"Is the fact that your father died in a fire the reason you're so intent on this case?" she asked, since the other questions weren't something she could answer.

"Not entirely."

She sat up, setting her wineglass aside. How had they ever gone down this road? Compartmentalizing her feelings for Wes was critical. Even he said she could find a way to keep their professional and personal lives separate.

Yeah, right.

But the investigator in her couldn't let the subject lie. "If not your father, then why? I know there's something personal in this for you."

"It's nothing."

She slid to the edge of the bed. "I shared the most profound pain of my life, and if you can't—"

"She dumped me, okay? I thought she cared about me, but then some guy with a Mercedes and a much bigger wallet comes along, and I'm history."

She turned to look at him over her shoulder. "Who dumped you? What are you—" She stopped, her heart kicking at her ribs as she leapt off the bed. "Dammit, Kimball, you're personally involved in this case up to your eyeballs."

"You knew that from the start."

"I knew you didn't like Addison. I thought maybe he cut you off in traffic one too many times. Or he beat you out of the starting quarterback position in high school. I didn't know he stole your girlfriend." She hadn't even considered this was about a woman.

Why hadn't she? Because her libido and her brain were all tangled together over Wes Kimball. Because he'd thrown her for a loop, and she was still dizzy and unfocused. She glared down at him. "You can't work this case."

He raised his eyebrows. "Excuse me?"

"You have a grudge against the victim—or primary suspect, depending on which version plays out." Pacing the length of the bedroom, she rubbed her temples. "If this ever does make it to court with Addison on the defense, his attorney would tear into the investigation like a hungry shark."

"The evidence will back up the case."

"Oh, thank you, Pollyanna." She wanted to kick something. Hard. Preferably him. She didn't see any point in reminding him how hard arson was to prove in the first place, much less with this complication added to the mix. Not to mention if Addison did get off, he'd probably then sue the crap out of Wes—and the city—in retaliation. She had to shut him out—for his own good as well as the case's.

He rose, standing in her path to stop her pacing. "I can still be objective."

She stared at him in disbelief. "You *must* be kidding."

"Look, it's in the past. I'll admit I don't like the guy, but I'm not about to manufacture evidence to convict him."

"That's comforting. And here I thought you were using this case to get back at him." *Using me,* she wanted to add, but didn't. No matter what personal closeness they'd shared, she had to keep this problem on a professional level.

Oh, yeah. Like you can do that while yelling at the man and dressed in your bathrobe.

He tunneled his hand through his hair. "Dammit, Cara, I'm a cop. I can separate—" He stopped, shook his head. "Okay, maybe I have a hard time separating my feelings from my cases. But *you* don't. You'll keep me straight."

She sank to the bed, her anger suddenly gone, leaving her drained. On top of all the ramifications this had for her case, she couldn't get the vision of Wes and this other woman out of her head. What had she meant to him? How did he feel about her now?

She felt deceived. By him and his brother. There were relationships and pasts in this town and its people that she knew nothing about. Ben had to know about this thing with Wes and Addison. Why had he suggested him as a liaison in the first place?

"You kept this from me," she said.

"I was supposed to introduce myself and say 'By the way, Addison and I shared the same woman'?"

She glared up at him. "Yes."

He glared back. "Fine, but you can't kick me off this case."

A chill raced through her blood. She kept her tone calm, without emotion. "Yes, I can."

"I can't believe you don't trust me."

"I don't know you."

Eyes blazing, he flung his hand toward the bed. "Then what was *that* about?"

"This isn't about sex. This is about the case. I don't know you professionally, and everything I've seen so far leads me to believe you can't be objective about Addison."

"And how do *I* know you won't let him charm his way to innocence?"

"How *dare* you question my integrity?"

"You questioned mine."

She pointed toward the door. "Get out."

"Gladly." He stomped toward the door. "But you're not throwing me off this case. I'll work alone if I have to."

She said nothing, just sat still and miserable on the bed. This whole argument was just further proof that she was lousy at relationships. She hadn't wanted a one-night stand, but it looked as though she'd gotten one. She jolted when he slammed the apartment door.

Then lay back and let the tears roll down her cheeks.

WES KICKED his desk—again. He'd screwed up—again.

He'd actually expected Cara to trust him. About a man he couldn't stand, when he'd made absolutely no effort to even consider for a second the man was innocent, when he hadn't even bothered to hide his bias.

He'd been humiliated and pissed when Bethany had left him. At first, he'd thought losing her was what brought about all the anger and pain. But eventually, he'd realized it was his pride. Addison was *not* a better man than he. He didn't long for her, he longed for retaliation.

Stupid. Just plain stupid.

Like they were two kids on the playground, each trying to fly higher on the swings.

He refused to withdraw from this case, though. He wanted to contribute. He knew this town, its people, better than her. He knew things about Addison that she couldn't, and might not ever find out about. Things he'd resisted detailing because, one, they might not be relevant, and two, because they might embarrass innocent people. And besides his own deep-seated sense of justice, he wanted this nut stopped. His brothers fought those fires. His hometown was threatened. And he had an opportunity to prove he belonged in his family. To make his father proud, had he lived to see Wes as a man.

But he had to get beyond the past. And quickly. Or he was going to lose his part in this case. He was going to lose Cara's respect. He probably already had.

A knock on the door saved him from his pity party.

Steve stuck his head inside. "Is it safe? I was warned to stay out of your path today."

Wes just grunted.

"I'll take that as a yes." His brother strode inside, plopping himself in the chair in front of Wes's desk. "So, how goes the investigating?" He waggled his eyebrows. "With the lovely Captain Hughes?"

Wes scowled.

Steve grinned. "That well, huh?"

"It's fine."

"Oh, it's *fine*. And I thought maybe you were having problems."

"What makes you say that?"

"Probably because you look like you'd rather punch me than talk to me."

Another knock. This time, Eric Norcutt peeked around the corner of the door. "Hey, man, wanna grab a beer after shift? The bar has a new video poker—"

"No!" Wes said.

"Damn, man. What's with you?"

Wes pointed at his always overflowing in-box. "I've got work to do, don't you?"

"Man, you *need* a beer." Norcutt leaned back, pulling the door closed.

Staring at Wes, Steve angled his head. "I'd like to echo that idea. And it might help to talk about things."

Miserable, Wes rubbed his temples. "I don't see how."

"Working with her has been that bad?"

"She's just so damn inflexible. And difficult."

"And beautiful, interesting and smart," Steve added.

Wes glared at his brother. "You're pretty observant." And he didn't like that idea one bit.

He shrugged. "She's a woman." Steve's gaze, so like his own, met Wes's. "So, what does she disagree with you about?"

It wasn't lost on Wes that Steve automatically assumed he'd called Cara inflexible and difficult because she didn't agree with him. "She found out about mine and Addison's recent personal history, and she wants to kick me off the case."

"Ah. Just how badly do you want to continue?"

He sighed. "I *need* this. Don't ask me why." But he acknowledged to himself that part of him couldn't help a lingering fantasy of having his family, his peers, even the mayor, pat him on the back. Part of him wanted to finally feel as if he deserved to be his father's son.

"Well then, you're going to have to prove to her you can be an investigator, not a jealous lover."

Wes set his jaw. "I'm *not* jealous of Addison."

"But you resent him, and you can't get past that to be objective, right?"

"I *know* he's guilty."

Steve shook his head. "At the risk of you calling me inflexible and difficult, you don't *know* anything. You *think* he's guilty. Do you have any evidence?"

"No, but—"

"Hell, Wes, you're a cop. Act like one."

Had that comment come from Ben, Wes would have argued. He'd have argued and been ticked off. But the quiet frustration on his normally genial younger brother's face had him pausing. Steve was only reiterating his own conclusions.

He had to get beyond the past.

"YOU DELIBERATELY didn't tell me about Addison and your brother's history," Cara accused, standing with her feet apart and braced for an argument on the other side of Ben Kimball's desk.

Ben's eyes flashed briefly, then he sighed, as if he'd known this moment would eventually arrive. "My brother and I don't always see eye to eye, but he's a great cop. He reads people well. He doesn't let anyone get away with anything, no matter who they are."

Cara nodded. She wasn't so angry that she could deny the lieutenant's strengths.

"He's worked with the county fire marshal for years on the arson cases," Ben went on. "He's accepted responsibilities and duties that he didn't have to in order to help us out. It's a small town, Cara, I don't have the manpower, or the need, for a full-time arson investigator."

Since she was already exhausted and miserable about the way she'd let her fight with Wes escalate, Cara concentrated on thinking of a return argument. She was aware of all the facts he'd just mentioned, but having them stated to her so calmly and proficiently made her want to sink into the chair beside her and admit her anger wasn't just professionally motivated. She'd lain awake last night, picturing Wes and this woman together—touching, laughing, sharing the same closeness and passion she'd just experienced with him. She felt intimately betrayed. And had no right to.

"More people than you or I must know about this conflict between Wes and Addison," she said finally. "It could compromise the investigation. Criminal prosecution isn't just about the facts. It's about *perception* of the facts."

Ben threw up his hands. "What else are we supposed to do? You won't find anyone in this town who doesn't know, who hasn't had some dealing with Robert Addison. No matter how he comes across, I knew my brother would be fair."

"He sure doesn't *act* fair."

"A risk I took, I realize, but I trust him. Ultimately, that's what it comes down to. I trust him with this case, with my life." He paused, his eyes going soft. "You can, too."

Cara spun away. "I'm not going there, Chief. This isn't about us."

"Is there an 'us' for the two of you?"

"No." Remembering the teasing, but hungry look on Wes's face last night, her heart squeezed tight, then released.

"Will you sit down? You look exhausted."

She found the strength to laugh and stared at him over her shoulder. "Why are you always telling me that?"

He extended his arm, inviting her to the chair opposite his desk. "Because it's always true. I'm a caretaker. Just ask my wife."

The mention of Monica had Cara moving forward. She dropped into the chair. "If you don't mind my asking, how the hell did the two of you get together?"

He grinned. "Quickly."

His smile reminded her of Baby Steve's charm. Even Wes's teasing smile had accompanied his comments about her love of Italian food, her devotion to exercise. God help any woman who came within a mile of these guys. "I'll bet."

And she suddenly felt steadier. Not necessarily better, or more comfortable about Wes or her case, but at least she wasn't imagining their faceless arsonist walking gleefully away from the courthouse.

Of course if that person was Robert Addison, she might be here for a month trying to prove her case. He'd conveniently forgotten to send her the names of the ladies who were supposedly his alibi. His secretary, sounding flustered, had said Mr. Addison was playing golf, but she'd relay the message. Cara was half tempted to march out to the ninth hole and—

Someone knocked on the door.

"Come in," Ben said.

A uniformed police officer shuffled in. Cara immediately recognized him as one of the cops from the scene of the warehouse fire. The lack of stripes and the hesitant expression on his face made her automatically think *rookie.*

"Sir. Ma'am." His throat moved as he swallowed. "I, uh…actually, I needed to speak to Ms., uh…Captain Hughes."

Even as Cara's pulse zoomed, Ben gestured to the chair next to her. "Sit down, Dave."

Dave shook his head. "I, uh, prefer to stand."

Just get to it! Cara wanted to shout. Dave obviously wasn't bringing good news. She'd seen that look on a law enforcement official's face too often not to recognize the signs.

"The thing is…" He drew a deep breath. "The glove piece is missing."

Ben looked at Cara, then at Dave. "The glove piece?"

Dave stared at the floor. "The one recovered at the fire the other night."

Cara's head spun. "What do you mean it's gone? It was sent to the state lab yesterday."

Slowly, Dave lifted his head. Regret and fear shown back at her. "No, ma'am, it didn't go with the other evidence, some foul-up in the paperwork. When the mistake was discovered, it was rescheduled for delivery this morning. But when the tech went to get it, it was gone."

Cara fought to take deep, even breaths. *Anything* but that scorched piece of latex.

Anything.

The texture of latex gloves had the unique ability to capture fingerprints. Sometimes they were too smudged to help with anything, but every once in a while, a perfect imprint of the user's prints appeared like a photograph, a conclusive link in the evidentiary chain.

Okay, maybe the gloves had meant nothing. The state health inspector could have thrown them down during a routine visit, a worker who didn't want a paper cut could have worn them, but just the *idea* of whose prints *might* have been captured, had Cara's blood boiling.

"How could this happen?" she asked in a too-soft, accusing whisper.

"I'm not sure, ma'am." Dave's brow wrinkled. "Everybody who comes through the evidence room is logged. The sergeant in charge says nothing's out of the ordinary."

"I want to talk to him," Cara said, standing. "I want to talk to everyone who's touched, or so much as stood within fifty feet of that evidence."

"Yes, ma'am."

Cara didn't want to flay the messenger. This wasn't Dave's fault. It was hers. This case was *her* responsibility. The buck stopped at her doorstep. She should have rented an independent storage facility, should have logged the evidence herself.

For a second, some horrible part of her wondered about Wes. She'd turned the evidence over to the police, to put in their storeroom, since the fire department didn't have their own. But no matter how much Wes might want Addison to be guilty, she knew he wouldn't take or alter evidence.

Maybe she did trust him, just a bit, after all.

Besides, Wes *wanted* Addison's prints on that glove. He probably thought they *were* on the glove. Taking it wouldn't help prove his theory in the least.

She forced her frustration to the pit of her stomach. "Get me that information, Dave. And when you have it, bring it to me. *Nobody* but me."

Dave actually clicked his heels together. "Yes, ma'am." He spared a brief glimpse for Ben, and, receiving a nod, turned and strode from the office.

"Wes wouldn't—"

Cara raised her hand to stop Ben's defense of his brother. "I know." She met the chief's gaze. An understanding, a resolve she hadn't expected, surged through her. "The question is—who did?"

8

WES STARED THROUGH the windshield of the gray sedan he'd borrowed from one of the dispatchers. He was exhausted, half-asleep, but trying to focus on the office building in front of him.

The surveillance wasn't much, but it was his small way of keeping his hand in the case. He'd picked up the phone dozens of times during the day to call Cara, to explain, apologize and push his need to stay part of the investigation.

But he hadn't. And the one time he might have seen her at the station, he'd been driving by a succession of properties owned by Addison, trying to decide which one to stake out. When he'd returned to the station, he'd heard about the missing glove and that a furious Captain Hughes had grilled everybody she could find, even calling in off-duty people when she didn't get the answers she wanted.

She'd probably find a way to blame the whole mess on him. Of course, he'd been quick to blame Addison, but quickly learned that Addison hadn't been anywhere near the station in the last two days. The obvious answer was a paid break-in, but they'd found no physical evidence to back that up. An inside job? Maybe. But Wes couldn't imagine any of his fellow cops doing anything like that.

So, for now, he was focusing on the next obvious target. He hoped to either prevent the next fire, or catch the arsonist in the act. If the arsonist was, in fact, Addison himself, he'd throw a freakin' party.

As he leaned his head back, imagining the pop of a champagne cork, the headlights of another car appeared briefly at the end of the side road he'd pulled off. He slumped down in the seat, his heart pounding as he waited for the car to pass.

Several minutes after the tires had crunched down the gravel road, he peeked out the windows. All was quiet.

Staring into the dark night, watching for any sign of movement near the building, a new aspect of the case suddenly occurred to him. His resentment of Addison had to be felt by others. It was possible that some nut really had targeted Addison. What if there was a guy out there who held a personal grudge? A guy whose moral code was somewhat more flexible than Wes's? What might that guy do?

Snap.

Wes ducked. He wrapped his hand around the revolver he'd stored under his seat. A twig snapping? The wind blowing a branch?

He didn't think so.

Somebody was out there.

Though the sound had come from behind him, and he couldn't risk raising himself high enough to look in the rearview mirror, he glanced out the open window into the side mirror. He could see the whole side of the car. Nobody was sneaking up on him.

Crunch.

The gravel road. Someone, or something, was definitely getting closer.

Then a semiauto pistol appeared over the front of the mirror. "That better be you slumped in that seat, Lieutenant."

Wes relaxed his tense muscles. "Cara."

She holstered the pistol, then knelt by the open window. "Figures we'd both pick the same building to stake out."

He ignored the way his heart picked up speed. "Figures." He paused, trying to decide whether to apologize for last night's fight, or pretend they were still just two officers working the same case. "Two pairs of eyes are better than one, I guess. Hop in." He leaned across the car and opened the passenger door.

As she slid inside, her gardenia-laden perfume filled the confined space. He inhaled deeply, figuring he'd better get the case talk out of the way first, since he wouldn't be too productive as a cop after extended influence under that scent.

"I guess you heard about the glove," she said, facing him and leaning her back against the door.

"Yeah. Any leads?"

"Nobody knows anything." She angled her head. "Kind of odd for a police department, don't you think?"

Even though he'd considered the same thing, he stiffened. "An inside job?"

Her aqua gaze connected with his. "I think so."

He sighed and gripped the steering wheel. "Instinct or evidence?"

"Evidence."

"Naturally."

"I'm not trying to start trouble, Wes. Everybody I've met seems professional and eager to solve the case."

"I thought you weren't too pleased with our welcoming committee."

"I don't blame them for resenting me. They don't trust outsiders. But there are no signs of a break-in. No picked locks on the evidence room door. Nobody unusual roaming about. I don't know what other conclusion to draw."

"I know. Believe it or not, I have considered this inside job idea."

"That's very..." She paused, then smiled slightly. "Open-minded of you."

"I'm working on it." He turned his head toward her. "Know what this means?"

"Hmm?"

"You need me. I'm inside the department. I know these people. I'll know if anybody's acting out of character."

"True."

"Unless, of course, you think I took the glove."

She looked away, then back. "I won't lie and say the idea didn't occur to me. But only for half a second and only because of the obvious connection—you work there. But I know that no matter how much you want Addison to be guilty, you wouldn't take that step."

Her opinion, her *belief,* in him meant way more than he wanted to acknowledge. "I've decided to be more open-minded about him, too."

She raised her eyebrows. "Really?"

"Really." He told her his theory about the nut with a vengeance who might be targeting Addison.

"That definitely fits with all the evidence—except the missing glove."

"Unless the nut's a cop."

She shook her head, as if she, too, didn't want to consider that possibility. "Unless."

Wes scanned the area around the office building again. "I'm sorry about last night," he said quietly, then turned to look at her. "I shouldn't have kept my history with Addison from you. It was unprofessional and unfair."

She pressed her lips together briefly. "It's my fault, too. I shouldn't have flown into such a tantrum. It just...caught me off guard."

He remembered the anger, but also the look of betrayal, in her eyes. This affair between them made every emotion seem heightened, every word and gesture heavier. He wanted to touch her, pull her into his arms, but he also understood the distance they needed to maintain on the job. "So, I'm back on the case?"

"I guess I do need you."

"You don't sound too excited about that."

"I'm grateful. I just—" She clenched her hand into a fist. "It's just weird, given the personal nature of our relationship."

Screw distance. He grinned and reached for her hand, tugging her against his chest. *"The personal nature of our relationship?"*

She settled herself in his lap, looping her arms around his neck. "Make fun of me, and I'll pull out my gun again."

"I guess I'd better behave then."

She slid her fingers through the hair at his temple. "You? Not a chance."

"Not a chance," he repeated, then leaned forward and captured her lips.

Kissing her, he poured out all his frustration—the mismatched pieces of the case, the need to be objective about Addison, the propriety that demanded they maintain a certain distance, the rebellious nature inside him that wanted to tear down those barriers.

She responded to his touch as if she was the match to his flame. Her tongue slid sinuously against his, enticing him, exciting him. His body hardened; his heart hammered.

Earlier today, there were times he really thought he might never touch her again. He hadn't wanted to acknowledge that his stubbornness might have cost him the most exciting woman he'd ever met, but now that he finally had her against him again, he could admit he didn't want to let go. Not now. Not—

Well, not for a very long time.

Her curves fit perfectly against him. Her mouth was heaven on earth.

How a woman could pull a gun on him one minute, then have his pulse soaring for an entirely different reason the next, he had no idea. But he wasn't arguing.

He was absorbing. Enjoying. Loving.

Gasping, she pulled back. "We do that very well."

He smiled. "We certainly do." He moved toward her again when she shook her head.

"Okay, Lieutenant, enough touchy-feely stuff." She scooted back to her side of the car. "Back to business."

His blood was still on full boil. "That wasn't near long enough a break."

"I'm not having sex with you in this car."

He fought to control the pounding insistence of his

body. He watched her smooth the wrinkles from her shirt. She rolled her shoulders, her face sliding into arson investigator mode.

Damn, she was something.

Her gaze seized his. "Now don't get all wound up about this, but I have a personal question to ask about this woman and Addison."

He angled his head. *"This woman?* You mean Bethany?"

Mockingly, she mouthed, *Bethany.* "That's her name?"

Just the idea that Cara obviously resented Bethany sent a warm blossom of pleasure up his spine. "She's nice."

Cara nearly snarled. "I'm sure."

Wes cleared his throat. "You wouldn't be, uh…jealous, would you?"

She glared at him. "Don't be ridiculous."

"I'll try."

Her glare intensified.

"Okay. I was goading. Sorry. I'll control myself from now on."

"I certainly hope so." She waved her hand, as if impatient to get back on topic. "What did Roland Patterson mean about Addison's sexual proclivities?"

He should have known even the smallest comment wasn't likely to get by the sharp captain. All this was as far into the personal realm as one could get without an M.D. and some type of probing device, but he also knew total honesty was the only choice. "Addison likes rough sex. Not rape," he quickly added. "There's a small group around that's into this domination and submission thing."

Her eyes widened. "In *Baxter?*"

He smiled. "It's always the quiet ones.... In any case, it seems to be consensual. At least I haven't found anyone who's complaining."

"Including this woman you dated?"

"*Especially* her."

Cara's gaze roved Wes's face. He seemed casual about this wild statement, yet there's no way the revelation could have been quite so easy. "She left you because you didn't want to be part of this sexual subculture?"

He shook his head. "Subculture gives it way too much significance. She was exploring that part of her sexuality, and I didn't feel comfortable there, so she found someone who did. I was hurt at first, mad and resentful. But I realized that was her prerogative. We didn't fit. I don't regret the loss."

The casual way he spoke about this woman gave Cara a measure of ease. She wished she could set aside this jealous, irrational woman who'd become part of her thoughts, but she couldn't. Wes and his attention to her had become way too important. "But you can't stand Addison."

"That stems from much more than her. After our breakup, I was angry and embarrassed. I dug into Addison—his past, his present—and I found a lot of things that didn't mesh with his perfect public image. The dom and sub thing is just a sideline. I learned he liked to chase married women." He shrugged, though the things he'd found out—broken marriages, kids without complete families—were hardly incidental. "He liked the challenge. He didn't much care who he hurt in the process."

The whole picture sickened her. "Well, damn, you could have told me this from the start."

"But how many innocents would it hurt? I don't want those women, their kids part of this case."

As much as her life revolved around her job, even Cara couldn't deny the humanity in that choice. "Agreed. We don't go there unless we absolutely have to."

"The big question for us comes down to one thing. Is Addison an arsonist or a victim?"

"I'd rather he was guilty."

"You? I thought we were being objective."

"We are." She stared at the floor. "But I understand why you're biased when it comes to Addison."

He leaned close. "Are you saying I was right?"

She glanced up, meeting his amused expression. "That would serve me right, wouldn't it? If you were right all along?"

He grinned. "If it's any consolation, I think you're right about the glove. I think someone in the police department contributed to the robbery."

She grabbed his thigh. "Who?"

His gaze dropped to her hand, and she realized how close they were now sitting, how the heat of his body suffused her palm. For a moment, she struggled to remember what they were talking about. The man affected her senses way too strongly. Working with him was both torture and a thrill.

"It could be a number of people," he said when he lifted his head. "Last year, an environmental group rolled into town, protesting the waste disposal procedures of Addison's lumber mill. They said the chemicals used to treat the wood were seeping into a nearby creek. Baxter PD had to rotate guards at the door of the mill to make sure the protests didn't get out of hand.

"After a few days, cops started talking about how they fish that creek with their kids. How the chemicals could give them cancer, affect the water supply. There were a lot of angry people."

"Angry at Addison?"

He nodded. "They blamed him."

"So, what happened?"

"EPA came in and inspected. They found a small leak in the chemical-carrying pipe that ran alongside the creek, but felt certain it hadn't been significant enough to affect water or the fish. It cost Addison a bunch of money to fix, of course. So, really, he was the only one who lost."

"Angry is one thing. Manslaughter and arson is an awfully big leap. You really think one of those cops decided Addison hadn't suffered enough and turned to arson?"

Wes's eyes looked bleak, but resigned. "No, but it's possible somebody was sympathetic enough to the arsonist's cause to help him out."

LATER, IN HER BED, Cara smiled and stretched, her body still echoing with pulses of Wes-induced pleasure. The man did indeed have many talents. She slid her hand around his neck. "I want you to tie me up."

"What?"

Since both of them were already bare-chested, with him lying on top of her in her bed, maybe she'd cheated a bit in making her request. "For purely investigative purposes, of course."

"You like that kind of stuff?"

"I wouldn't know." She shifted her body, so that he lay between her legs. He groaned respectfully, and she smiled. He hadn't wanted to push this button with Bethany, but both the investigative and personal parts of her wanted to explore this angle of sexuality. "I just want to know what it's about. Don't you? Don't you wonder if they're just weirdos, or if you're missing out on something great?"

"No. Yes. No."

She kissed the sensitive spot at the base of his throat. "Oh, come on. It could be fun."

He still looked wary. "Where's your gun?"

"Holstered. I think I dropped it in the hall on our way in here."

"You *think?*"

She sighed. "Good grief. This isn't about violence. It's about intimacy. Trust."

"And you trust me?"

"With my body and personal safety? Absolutely. Now where are your handcuffs?"

He actually went pale. "I'm *not* handcuffing you."

"Fine, but I don't have any silk scarves."

He sat back, then slid off the bed. Immediately, Cara felt the coldness of his retreat. She'd been partially teasing him, but intently curious about this level of closeness. Now, she just felt ridiculous.

He paced beside the bed. "You really want to do this?"

She stared at the ceiling. "Only if you do."

He paced and said nothing.

Then, finally, he sat on the edge of the bed. His gaze searched hers, forcing her to meet him head-on.

"I talked to a lot of people involved in this kind of thing. It's not something you take lightly. People can get hurt. It's a wobbly moral issue. You can feel scared, overwhelmed, smothered."

Not breaking their gazes, she sat up, sliding her hand down his side, admiring the lean muscles, the manliness of his body. "You've never had those kind of fantasies?"

"A little, I guess. But I don't get off using women."

"It's just pretend." The scent of him, the heat of him, had her heart hammering. The idea they could indulge, that she felt comfortable enough to take this step, had her both excited and scared. She leaned close, pressing a kiss to the side of his neck, the center of his chest.

Beneath her lips, his pulse skipped a beat. "You're seducing me," he said.

"I'm trying."

"You're succeeding."

"Come on, Wes," she whispered in his ear, punctuating her meaning by trailing her hand down the front of his jeans, "we'll even have a quit word."

He sucked in air between his teeth. "Like what?"

"If either one of us doesn't want to continue we'll say..."

"Elvis."

In the process of kissing his jawline, she stopped. "Elvis?"

"That's the word."

Smiling, she squeezed his erection. "Fine by me. Let's go."

He surprised her by immediately looming over her, pinning her arms above her head. His bright blue eyes burned. "You'll do everything I say."

Part of her—the part that loved to control things, to be in charge—rebelled instantly.

No, no, it insisted.

She doused the feeling. She wanted this closeness with him, wanted to know a new aspect of their desire.

"I'll do everything you say," she said, trailing her hand through his hair.

He reached toward the floor, returning with her shirt. Quickly, with a wince he couldn't seem to hide, he looped the arms around her wrists, tying her to the bedpost.

Her arms immediately felt heavy. *Trapped.*

She swallowed the urge to tear her wrists from the bindings, which, with a slight tug, she was sure she could have broken. But then that was the whole idea, wasn't it? Knowing you could escape, but not wanting to.

She also became suddenly aware of the nakedness of her upper body. His gaze roved her from neck to waist. She still had on her jeans and panties, but she had the feeling those barriers would soon disappear.

Given his initial reluctance, she encouraged him by arching her back.

His face appeared above hers. "Don't." He laid his warm palm across her stomach and pressed her back to the mattress. "I'm in charge, remember?"

As he smiled, she shivered. She had no fear, but was sure he'd make her pay for any wrong moves. She simply nodded.

Flicking the button on her jeans, he slid his fingers beneath the waistband of her undies—her thin, mesh, black undies. His touch reminded her of her visit that afternoon to his sister's lingerie shop, where Cara had rapidly, looking over her shoulder, purchased her first pair of thong underwear from Skyler's assistant. Maybe that act alone had started her down this road of sensuality. Maybe she'd been longing for this level of closeness all along.

But then his index finger teased the top of her feminine folds, and she forgot all about why she was here, just that she was.

He hooked his thumbs beneath the waistband of her jeans, jerking them down in one, swift, masterful move.

She closed her eyes and arched her back.

Sitting on her thighs, he moved his hands from her shoulders to her hips, sliding one finger under her panties, across the core of her desire. "These are nice."

She licked her lips. Her body was on fire and didn't feel capable of much of a response. "They're new."

His thumb rubbed against her nub. "For me?"

"Mmm... *Yes.*"

"Turn over."

Her eyes popped wide. "What?" Then she saw the intent expression on his face and remembered her role. "Yes. Sir."

He untied her wrists briefly, allowing her to roll over, then his voice whispered in her ear, "You're very good, my love. Every time you call me *sir* I'll give you a reward."

She turned her head sideways, sighing as he settled his weight across the back of her thighs. "What kind of reward?"

In answer, he trailed his finger beneath her panties.

She held her breath. Her body throbbed. Her muscles contracted. Moisture dampened her legs. "That's a good reward."

He grabbed the top edge of her panties. Then he ripped them apart. "It gets better."

As she gasped for air, he laid his bare chest across her back, his lips teasing the edge of her ear, the nape of her neck. Heat suffused her skin, her blood. She had to concentrate on drawing air into her lungs.

His hands gripped her hips, holding her in place as his mouth continued the pleasurable assault on her neck. The fact that she couldn't see him was an illicit thrill. His hands seemed bigger, the hot breath rushing across her skin seemed harsh.

Then his fingers slid into the dampness between her thighs. She groaned.

"Like that?" he whispered against her ear.

"Yes, sir."

He slid one finger inside her, teasing, pressing, then withdrawing. His thumb flicked down her folds, just brushing the center of her desire.

Even as her pulse spiked, she moaned with frustration.

"Faster?" he asked.

"Yes, sir."

He obliged, and her hands, caught in the bindings above her head, throbbed.

"Deeper?" he asked, still in that abrasive, somehow unfamiliar voice.

She was on the edge and fairly certain another moment or two of his fabulous hands would send her over. "*Please,* sir."

To her utter shock, he withdrew his hands completely. Before she managed a word of protest, he briefly loosened the knots around her hands, flipped her over, then tightened them again.

As she glared up at him, his face—flushed with arousal—hovered over hers; his blue eyes blazed with barely retrained passion. "Not so fast. And not without me."

In seconds, he'd stripped off his jeans and rolled on protection. She lay on the bed, watching him with a mixture of anticipation and desperation. His swift retreat, with her so close to exploding, had magnified her hunger ten-fold. And she still hadn't forgotten the confines of her trapped arms. Her muscles tingled in protest of their odd position.

But there were other parts of her much more needy.

When he returned to the bed, he took only a second to brace his weight, then he surged inside her body. She arched her back and neck.

He held himself still for what seemed like an eternity. Her muscles tightened. Her heart pounded.

She angled her hips, squeezing him with her inner muscles for encouragement.

He said nothing and didn't move.

"Wes?"

"I think I'm supposed to be in better control," he said, his voice shaky, but his body still. "And you're supposed to beg."

"I'm supposed to *what?*"

Inside her, his erection throbbed. "Just do it already!"

"Please, please, please, s—"

He moved. Oh, boy did he move. Quickly, as if adrenaline had just shot through his veins. She would have sighed in relief if she could have drawn a decent breath.

It felt odd to not be able to hold on to him. Trying not to break rhythm, she managed to wrap her legs around his thighs. The movement forced him deeper and brought simultaneous groans from them both.

She shot to the rise quickly, pulsing pleasure shooting through her veins, her muscles, her very soul. She shouldn't want him this much, *need* him this much. She definitely shouldn't fall for him.

But she was almost certain it was too late.

WITH THE LAST BIT of strength he had, Wes reached up and untied the shirt around Cara's wrists.

She stretched her arms upward. "Thanks."

Still trying to draw full breath, he flopped onto his back.

"You owe me twenty bucks, by the way," she said.

"For what?"

"I bought those panties in your sister's shop today."

"*One* pair for twenty bucks? That's robbery."

"Tell me about it."

"I'll get you a refund. They were clearly not tear resistant."

She laughed. "Lucky for you."

He smiled. He really liked that he could laugh with her, even after an intense sexual experience. "Are you okay?"

"I'm great."

He glanced over at her. He'd started out protesting this whole tying-up business, but he had to admit he'd enjoyed the fantasy of having her body all to himself, of teasing and withdrawing. "You're sure?"

She turned her head, meeting his gaze. "It was exciting, the sexual need mixed with a little fear, the inability to move very much."

"But..."

"But I couldn't imagine indulging on a regular basis and certainly not casually. Anybody who gets off on true fear is disturbed. You'd have to really trust your partner."

His pulse jumped. "I guess this means you trust me."

"I already said I did."

"But that was when you were after my body."

She lifted her hand, cupping his cheek in her palm. "So I'm saying it again. I trust you—with my body and this case."

He noticed she didn't mention her heart. But he didn't want that complication anyway. Their arrangement was perfect—temporary pleasure, companionship and a challenging case as a bonus. She didn't want anything more. Neither did he.

She was beautiful and smart. Her passion for her job, her need to find justice made his body melt. They had great chemistry. But that was all. Simple. Direct. Temporary.

"I should probably go," he said, though he made no move to leave.

She scooted toward him, laying her head on his chest. "Stay. Stay the night."

He tucked his arm behind her, holding her tight as he closed his eyes, hoping he wasn't lying to himself.

Since he was very afraid he did want more.

9

RINGING FILLED HIS EARS.

Wes groaned and pulled Cara tighter against him. It couldn't be morning yet. "Turn off the alarm," he mumbled against her shoulder.

She sat up. "That's not my alarm clock. It sounds like a phone."

Wes buried his face in the pillow. "Let the machine get it."

"What if it's another fire?"

"Burn, baby, burn."

"Cute." She swatted him, and he felt her weight leave the mattress.

Turning onto his back, he pried open his eyes—more to get a look at her naked body as she moved across the room than any real curiosity about the source of the ringing. Hips swaying, she stalked around the end of the bed. Her creamy skin glowed beneath the stream of moonlight peeking through the bedroom window blinds.

Curves like those ought to be illegal.

She bent over, and his heart threatened to jump from his chest. "It's your cell phone."

He laid his hand over his racing heart. "You'll have to answer it." Then immediately realized what a bad idea that was. He bolted upright. It could be Ben or the mayor. The woman had made him completely lose his mind.

"Hello?" she said before he could grab for the phone. Then she paused, listening. "Hold on." She crawled onto the bed, extending the phone toward him.

Her face had lost its soft, sleepy, sensual look, replaced by Captain Serious. When he found this damn arsonist, he was personally going to punch the jerk in the mouth. "This better be good," he said into the phone.

"Lieutenant Kimball?" an unfamiliar, male voice asked.

"That's me."

"We need to talk."

He waited a beat. "We are talking."

"In person."

Now that he knew this wasn't a call to work, he was fast moving from mildly irritated to pissed. "Who the hell is this?"

"You can call me George."

"Are you going to make this phone call worth my aggravation anytime soon, George?"

"I've got some information for you about Robert Addison."

Wes froze, then waved his hand at Cara to come closer. He held the phone away from his ear slightly, so she could hear the caller.

"Got your attention now?" George asked, sounding amused.

"Yep. What do you know about Addison?"

"Stuff you want to, but we have to do this in person."

"Why?"

"I have proof."

Wes glanced at Cara, then at the clock—2:00 a.m. Gift horses named George who called in the early hours of a Saturday morning? Suspicious didn't even begin to cover it.

"Ten minutes, the park on Main Street," George said. "I won't wait."

"But—"

The phone went dead.

While he let loose a stream of curses, Wes glanced at the screen. The phone number on the caller ID told him the call had been made locally, but he didn't recognize it.

"No Southern accent," Cara said, sliding into her jeans. "Midwestern, maybe. Did he sound like anybody you know?"

"No." Wes punched in the number of the police station, then grabbed his own jeans while the call connected. "Roy, run a trace on this number." After he listed off the numbers, he told Roy the information was urgent and he'd hold.

"This could be the break we need," Cara said, striding into the hall, presumably for the rest of her clothes.

Wes waited until she returned before he spoke. She was going to be ticked off, but fear for her had his heart racing just a little too fast, his mind spinning just a few too many gruesome scenarios. "The guy asked *me* to meet him, Cara. I don't think he'd appreciate me bringing along a partner."

In the process of slipping into her shoulder holster, Cara went still. Her angry gaze captured his. "I'm not going *with* you. I'm following you. He won't even know I'm there."

He tossed on his shirt and groped under the bed for his boots. "You're not going."

"I'm not arguing about this with you, Lieutenant. I *am* going."

Sitting on the bed, he glowered at her as he tugged on his boots. "Have you ever noticed that when you want to push me away, you use my title instead of my name?"

She stood in front of him, arms crossed over her chest, feet planted firmly apart. "Just reminding you who's in charge."

"This could be dangerous."

"Which is why I'm going. You might need backup."

He stood, grabbing her arms. "Dammit, Cara, I—"

"I'm going regardless, so you might as well get over it."

He wanted to fold her into his arms, to hold her close and protect her. She was as well trained as he, probably better, but just the thought of her being within a mile of this meeting had everything inside him violently protesting.

"Wes, you still there?" The voice came from the phone Wes had dropped on the bed.

Wes scooped up the cell. "I'm here, Roy. What did you find out?"

"It's the phone booth at Main and Park. You need anything else?"

"No. Thanks." Wes disconnected, giving Cara only a passing glance as he strode from the room. "Stay out of sight, and be careful."

She stalked out of the apartment behind him, no doubt still angry he'd tried to keep her from going. She was a strong, independent woman, used to making her own decisions. He should have kept his mouth shut. He had no right to be overprotective.

But all that cold logic just didn't seem to matter.

He led them toward the park, her following behind him in her car. He couldn't help glancing continually in the rearview mirror. Panic had his hands shaky and his stomach hollow.

At least she had that pistol. He just prayed she wouldn't have to use it.

As he drove the last few blocks, her car turned off. He punched in her cell number. "Anything weird happens, you fire a shot in the air. I'll be there."

"Yes, Dad."

"Just watch your backside. I sorta like it."

She said nothing for a moment. "You, too." Then she disconnected.

By the time he approached the park, he was calmer. Cara was a professional. She was smart and quick. She'd be fine.

He wished he had a recorder, but that equipment was at the station, and he couldn't have risked the time to get it. George, no doubt, had planned it that way.

As he pulled the car along the deserted curb, he scanned the park for any movement. Almost to the corner, directly beneath a streetlight, was a bench. A blond-haired man sat there, dressed in khakis and a jean jacket, his arm lying casually across the back.

Relief surged through him. Visions of a street thug lurking in the shadows, a knife clutched firmly in his hand, faded. He seriously doubted he'd have to threaten this guy, or defend himself against him. Maybe this whole thing really was legit.

But he'd have to seriously talk to George about his lousy timing.

Still, he checked his service revolver before he got out of the car and looked over the area as he walked toward the bench. He hoped Cara kept her lovely butt planted and safe.

George eyed him carefully as he approached. "Evening, Lieutenant."

Wes sat on the far end of the bench. He judged George at about his same age, height and weight. He noticed, though, that his blond hair was white-blond and his face olive-toned. The opposites didn't fit, as if he'd dyed his hair. He seemed relaxed and confident, though. What was up with this guy? "Actually, it's morning."

"True." George's dark brown gaze met Wes's. "I understand Robert Addison is being investigated for these arsons."

Wes simply nodded.

"If you let it go a couple more weeks, the problem will solve itself."

"How's that?"

"Men he owes a great deal of money to—men other than my boss—aren't what you'd call patient."

His long-held suspicions just confirmed, Wes stifled the urge to jump up and dance. "He's in deep."

"If he doesn't produce some serious cash ASAP, he can make his final arrangements."

Loan sharks, maybe even the mob. Addison had certainly pissed off the wrong people. Like *that* was a big shocker.

George, however, didn't look much like a leg breaker. He looked more like an underwear model. "How do you know all this?"

"He owes my boss. We run a legitimate business, and we cut off Addison a while back. After dealing with us, it seemed Addison grew more desperate. We learned this because my boss engaged in some less-than-legal activities at one time. So, he knows people who know people, if you can buy that cliché."

Who *was* this articulate, well-dressed guy? And why did Wes have the feeling there was no boss? "And these people he knows are putting pressure on Addison?"

"So heavy he's suffocating."

Had he been right? Was Addison setting these fires for the insurance money?

Of course, George's story—if it was true—had also added another possibility. Maybe these loan sharks were setting the fires. Maybe they knew the insurance was the only way they'd get their money.

"You said on the phone you have proof," Wes said. "Where is it?"

As George reached into the pocket of his jeans jacket, Wes stiffened. He moved his hand toward his gun, but George pulled out a Ziploc bag. Inside was a piece of paper—about six-by-eight inches. "Open the bag and take the slip. By the edges only." When Wes did, George returned the bag to his pocket.

Wes realized George was protecting possible prints, both on the paper and his own on the bag. He stared at the paper now in his hands. It was an IOU for a hundred-thousand dollars.

"It's signed and dated," George pointed out. "Bottom right."

And, there, in glorious, clear black ink was a date eighteen months ago and Robert R. Addison's signature.

No, it wasn't a signed confession. And it didn't cover near the amount Addison was worth, but it would certainly put a nice dent in the golden boy's image. Loans R Us—the company on the IOU—was undoubtedly not endorsed by the FDIC.

Wes pinned George with his stare. "Loans R Us? How do I know this is legit?"

"Have the signature examined." He smiled slightly. "And then there's always the possibility a print or two will pop up."

As Wes's heart picked up speed, he had the feeling George *knew* a print had been preserved.

George rose. "I was never here. That will get you started. The rest you have to get on your own."

"If you give me this, you'll never get your money."

"I have a copy. Whether he goes to jail, or goes—" he looked downward "—my boss has claims he can file against the estate."

George turned away.

Wes figured the only way to find out who the guy really was, or his connection in all this, was to pull his gun. And he'd just been too damn *decent* for that kind of thanks. "One last question." When George turned back, Wes asked, "Why are you doing this?"

He shrugged. "A friend convinced me to follow my conscience."

As he walked away, Wes suddenly realized the end of this case might be within his grasp. But the possibility didn't bring him joy. Or satisfaction.

It only meant Cara would be leaving sooner.

"THIS IS A seriously generous gift," Cara said, her eyes narrowed on the bagged-for-evidence IOU.

"Yep."

"I don't trust seriously generous gifts."

"Me, either. But, call me crazy, I believed George." He shrugged. "Mostly anyway."

Cara tapped her fingers against the steering wheel. "He didn't look like a loan shark to me."

"Oh, but it's his *boss* who was the loan shark."

She smiled at Wes's sarcastic tone. "Oh, golly, I forgot."

"So, is it the loan sharks or Addison setting the fires?"

"A toss-up, I guess." She paused, considering. "But, if it's one of them why make the fires so obvious?

"It's as you said, the arsonist likes the excitement."

"Still, it's hard to make that fit with a professional job. If he'd been more clever, we might have believed it was just an accident. Even with more than one fire, weeks could have gone by before an investigator was brought in."

"Remember the arrogance of our guy. He doesn't believe he'll be caught. He's possibly got someone inside the police station. He's above the law."

"Or—if you buy the mob angle—outside it." She sighed. "What about George?"

Wes angled his body toward her, drawing her attention to his broad chest, reminding her of the texture and taste of his skin.

Wow, Cara, three whole minutes of investigative conversation before you thought of him and sex in the same sentence. That must be some kind of record.

She was disgusted with her lack of focus, her knee-weakening hunger for him. This was how people lost cases and ruined careers.

"As the arsonist?" Wes asked, shaking his head. "Doesn't fit."

Cara agreed. George, with his relaxed posture and tailored clothes, might be arrogant, but she didn't see a guy who preserved fingerprints and carried Ziploc bags in his pocket as reckless. And their arsonist most definitely had a reckless streak. "Maybe we'll find out more about him when I run his picture through the state and federal crime computers."

"And just how are you going to do that?"

She pulled a mini digital camera out of her jacket pocket and waved it at him. "Isn't technology wonderful?"

His eyes widened.

"The light was lousy, and this camera doesn't have much of a zoom, so the image is going to be small. But the techs in Atlanta can do wonders with fuzzy, dark pictures."

"He'd changed his hair, though. Maybe other features."

She shrugged. "It's worth a shot."

"Pretty quick thinking on your part."

"That's why they pay me the big bucks." She returned the camera to her pocket, deciding she'd e-mail it to the lab as soon as she got back to her apartment, and considered all they'd learned that night. Yesterday, she'd wondered if Addison was an arsonist or a victim. It was looking more and more as though he fell into the first category. "So when are you going to say I told you so?"

Wes grinned, making the shadowed scruffiness of his face even more appealing. "Would I do that?"

"Yes."

He shook his head. "Not until after he's behind bars. If it comes to that. We still have an odd angle that doesn't seem to fit anywhere—the missing glove."

"We need to check out the connections to this environmental group in the morning. You should talk to all the cops who were angry. And find out if anyone has a particular grudge against Addison."

"It's Saturday. And tomorrow's Sunday."

She raised her eyebrows. "The police station's closed on weekends?"

"No, but..." He trailed the tips of his fingers across her cheek. "I was hoping we could take some time off...together."

She swallowed; her body flooded with warmth. A whole weekend with Wes?

She should immediately say no, absolutely not. She should remind him of the evidence that needed to be processed for fingerprints. She should remind him they needed to continue their stakeouts—at *separate* Addison properties, even though Addison's long list of holdings made the exercise pretty futile. She should remind him of Mayor Collins's upcoming election, his brother's reputation as a fire chief, his own integrity as an investigator.

But the weak side of her, the side that wanted him to sleep beside her in her bed, the side that made her heart hammer in fear during his entire meeting with George, the side that couldn't concentrate on work for longer than a few minutes at a time, reminded her their time was short. The closer they got to finishing this case, the quicker their time together would end.

She wrapped her arms around his neck. "I can spare a few, productive hours."

MONDAY MORNING, Cara followed up—with little success—on George the Generous, then tackled Addison's alibi. As promised by his secretary, he'd finally e-mailed her the names and numbers of his liaisons over the weekend.

The woman he'd had dinner with readily admitted the date, and that he'd dropped her off at her house at midnight, both nights. The woman he'd spent the night with, however, was less than forthcoming.

"I really can't talk now," Sherri Hammond whispered into the phone.

"When can you?" Cara pressed.

"I—" She broke off as a crash echoed in the background, then the unmistakable sound of children's laughter filled Cara's ears.

A single mom? That didn't seem like Addison's style. "Ms. Hammond, are you all right?"

"Yes. I— Hold on a sec." She spoke sharply to someone, then she said, "I can't get away today."

"I'll come to you. I've got your address right here."

"No, I can't—"

"Are you alone? Other than the kids?"

"Yes, but—"

"I'll be there in ten minutes."

Cara grabbed her jacket and jumped in the car. She had no desire to ruin anyone's life, but with Addison looking more suspicious by the minute, she had to verify his whereabouts.

When she pulled up to the modest brick ranch house, she swallowed regrets and rolled her shoulders. A trim blonde, who looked about thirty, opened the door to her knock. She was pale, and her hand shook as she brushed her hair off her face and stepped back, allowing Cara into the foyer.

"Can we hurry? I put in a tape for my kids, but it won't keep them busy for long."

Cara heard singsong voices coming from the other room, but she focused on the woman in front of her. "I just need a minute, Mrs. Hammond." The woman flinched, and Cara added, "You are married, aren't you?"

She bowed her head. "Yes."

It wasn't her place to judge, but Cara had the strong urge to shake the woman. She was risking her marriage and family over Robert Addison?

Not your business.

She kept her voice matter-of-fact as she asked, "Were you with Robert Addison last Monday night until 6:00 a.m. Tuesday?"

"Y-yes, but I fell asleep about two. He was…gone when I woke up…around six-thirty."

"And also this past Monday night? Until one?"

She looked up, her eyes bleak as she nodded. "Please don't— My husband doesn't know."

"Thank you, ma'am. That's all." Cara turned, wrapping her hand around the doorknob. "He's not worth it," she said quietly. Then she jogged down the steps and to her car.

She'd just opened the door when a patrol car passed her on the street, then turned into the Hammonds' driveway. She frowned. No one else had the names of the women Addison had given her. She'd given him her personal e-mail address. How—

"Can I help you?" the officer called as he walked toward her.

"No, I just—" She slammed to a halt as the sun caught his brass nameplate. *Officer Hammond*. She knew him—or at least had seen him. At Addison's office the other day. He was the other moonlighting cop with Eric Norcutt.

"I was just leaving," she finished.

He grabbed her arm. "This is about those fires."

"I can't discuss my case, Officer." And, dammit, she didn't want to silence the laughter in that little house behind her.

"You keep my wife's name out of this," he said, squeezing her arm.

Cara pulled out of his grip and stepped back. "That sounded oddly like a threat."

His eyes blazed with anger. "Addison won't ruin my family."

He knows. Pity and suspicion welled-up inside her. "I'll do what I can."

As she pulled away from the curb, she realized the investigation had two new problems. Their prime suspect had an alibi. And another suspect had just been added to the list.

THAT AFTERNOON Wes found her at the firehouse, working in the office/bedroom reserved for the female firefighters.

He wasn't going to lie—exactly.

He was just leaving out details and suspicions he couldn't prove. How often had people—Cara included—reminded him he needed something more than his gut instincts to drive a case?

After spending part of Sunday and all this morning talking to cops about Addison, the grudges they might have had against him and the all-important missing glove, he was sick of suspicion, especially of people he'd thought he could trust. Several things just didn't add up. Or maybe they did.

Early in the afternoon, he'd visited the county crime lab, getting the fingerprints on the IOU analyzed, so he had plenty of legitimate details to give Cara. Sharing his feelings—about their relationship or the case—seemed premature, if not an outright waste of time.

But as he approached the open door to her makeshift office, he heard her voice as she spoke to someone on the phone, and his chest grew tight anyway. His deepening feelings for her were something he couldn't ignore much longer.

You're lousy at relationships, he reminded himself. He rarely even got along with his own brother.

It didn't take a psychiatrist to realize that after losing his father so young, he'd distanced himself from people he cared about. For him, love caused pain and worry. And he tended to be overbearing and controlling to compensate. Not a good combination with any woman, much less someone as independent as Cara.

And was he even in love with Cara? He thought he'd been in love with women before, but none of those relationships had worked out. How did he know that's what he was feeling now? Was there a *bang* moment when you just *knew?* Did you just say it and hope it was true? He'd barely known her a week, though they'd spent the last several nights together. He couldn't possibly be in love.

Shoving all that aside for the moment, he rapped on the door frame with his knuckles.

Sitting at the desk, she looked up, then waved him toward the chair in front of her. "Yes, sir, I understand," she said into the phone, "but I can't take much time right now. This case is ready to pop." She paused, listening, and Wes sat, taking a moment to admire her profile and the wispy strands of hair she hadn't managed to tuck behind her ear. Finally, she sighed. "Yes, sir. I'll drive down in the morning. E-mail me the file today."

When she dropped the phone in its cradle, Wes said, "Looks like you're in high demand."

Was it his imagination, or did her eyes brighten as they met his? "Atlanta FD needs a consult."

He leaned forward, bracing his forearms on the desk, inhaling the luscious, feminine scent of her. "It's tough being the best."

She gave him the grin he expected, and his heart gave him a swift kick at the results. "Isn't it though?"

After casting a quick glance at the open door to make sure no one was looking, he drew his thumb across her jawline. "You wanna go…out later?"

She angled her head. "Out? Like a date?"

"Yeah." It suddenly occurred to him they'd been intimately involved but had never actually been out together. They were either working or in bed. How cheap and stupid was that? No wonder he didn't have many successful relationships in his life.

"Sure, but it has to be early. I need to be on the road to Atlanta by six."

He coughed. "In the morning?"

"Yes, Mr. Lazy."

"When are you coming back? We need you here." He resisted adding, *I need you here.*

"I'll be back tomorrow night, though it might be late, depending on how much evidence there is to sort through." She glanced over his shoulder, then she leaned close and pressed her lips briefly to his. As she leaned back, her eyes were definitely brighter—even aroused—though her words were all business. "What have you got for me on Addison and the missing glove?"

"A mess." He rose and shut the door, knowing the temptation of him and Cara being this close, with a bed so handy was probably a bad idea, but the subject demanded absolute discretion. "Everybody's got opinions—all of them strong and on both sides."

"That's not a surprise, is it?"

"No, it just makes motives even more murky." He paced in front of the desk. "Some people think Addison is a cool guy, contributes to the local economy, always around to chip in for fund-raisers and buy a hard-working cop a drink." Remembering her comment of *he would be a fairly charming dinner companion,* he raised his eyebrows and sent an accusing look in her direction. "The two female dispatches, incidentally, fall into that category. Others still blame him for the lumber mill fiasco. They think he's fake and manipulative."

Cara propped her chin on her hand. "Addison is certainly a man with many faces. He contributes to local charities, then he probably has affairs with the married women running them."

"He's a quality guy," Wes added sarcastically. "But my interviews didn't tell me much I didn't already know. Nobody I spoke to looked particularly guilty or uncomfortable. Some of the guys still resent him for the chemicals he dumped in the creek, but I eliminated people, rather than added to the list of possible accomplices." One guy made his gut twist, but gambling wasn't a crime, even though debts certainly seemed to be driving Addison.

It could be nothing. You don't know. *Let the evidence play out. Check his story. Let Cara form an opinion without your interference.*

"There were a few inconsistencies that bothered me," he couldn't help adding, "but I'm checking on those."

"What do you know about Officer Hammond?"

"David?" He shrugged. "He's in the category of guys who aren't real wild about Addison."

"I guess so. His wife is having an affair with him."

His jaw dropped. "They've been married nearly ten years. They have two little kids." He tunneled his hand through his hair. "Does he know?"

"Yep."

"Man, I can't imagine—" This whole case made him absolutely sick. "He had access to the evidence room," he forced himself to admit. "Still, he just doesn't seem like the type."

"Your gut says no?"

"As a matter of fact, it does."

"*Addison won't ruin my family*—his exact words to me."

He winced. "Where was he during the fires?"

"On duty, which is why his wife was able to hook up with Addison."

"Which isn't any kind of alibi. He could have patrolled anywhere." What a mess. Asking his fellow officers leading questions, wondering if one of them had thrown away their career and moral code to help Addison, was bad enough. But to have a cop actually behind the whole thing— "Wait. This means Addison has an alibi."

Cara smiled. "I was wondering when that would hit you. Actually, though, he only has a partial alibi. On the night of the first fire, she fell asleep around two, didn't wake up until after six."

"I didn't get called to the scene until after three. He had plenty of time to set the fire."

"For this last fire, though, he didn't have time."

"But thanks to that missing glove we already know he had help."

She nodded in acknowledgement. "So Addison stays on the list, and Hammond goes on the list. At the top."

"At the top," he agreed, though the idea didn't set well to say the least. "What did you find out about our selflessly giving loan shark George?"

Her eyes narrowed. "Zip."

"Zip? As in you haven't found anything yet, or as in no record?"

"As in no record. I checked federal criminal databases, as well as state sources. Nothing about him pops."

"Not even a driver's license?"

"Nothing."

Wes considered their generous informant's odd hair color. "He'd changed his appearance."

"No doubt. But usually you can still find something that strikes a similarity. We're dealing with sophisticated computer-generated models that can notate something as obscure as ear shape. This guy is either really clean or is really smart."

"Or both."

"Yeah, right."

Wes smiled. "You can't be both?"

"Not in my experience. What about the IOU? Did the lab find any prints?"

"Addison's."

Her sea-green eyes gleamed. "Really?"

"Yep. There are a few smudged ones, as well."

"Presumably our friend George, or his 'boss.'"

"I guess. None of this means anything, of course, if Addison's innocent. But if this gets to court, we've got evidence to back up our case."

"It certainly makes George the Invisible Man's story seem more credible."

Wes rounded the desk, his thigh brushing the arm of her chair. He looked down, trying to ignore the rapid beat of his pulse, the needy, clawing sensation that invaded his body whenever he was this close. "So where does this leave us?"

"Hoping for a break."

He laid his hand on her shoulder, then slid his palm down her arm. "And where are we?"

She raised her gaze to meet his. "Oddly close."

"Why oddly?"

"I've told you before I don't mix my professional life with my personal one. I usually have a lot more focus. So, that's odd. And there's a lot still to do with this case. I should be devoting all my time there. We're also physically…close. Like now." She looked again toward the door. "It feels forbidden."

He dropped to his knees beside her, turning her swiveled chair and moving his body between her legs. "That's not such a bad thing."

"It could be for my career. I've worked long and hard to prove I deserve my job, Wes. I don't want anything to mess that up."

I'm not sure you're worth the risk, in other words. Even though he understood her reasoning and could identify with the need to prove herself better than anybody, her words hurt anyway.

"I won't let that happen." He slid his hands along her legs to her hips, pulling her to the edge of the chair. His waist pressed against the apex of her thighs. His erection pulsed. When he was this close to her, touching her amazing body, absorbing her endless energy, he knew he'd never get enough. She meant more to him than anyone in his life ever had. She excited him, challenged him…completed him.

She laid her hands on his shoulders. Her head dropped back. "Please, Wes. We need to work."

Smiling, he took advantage of her bared skin and kissed her throat. "I've worked. Frankly, I'm exhausted."

Her head popped up; her eyes bore unmistakable disappointment. "You are?"

He bit her ear lightly. "Maybe not."

10

CARA PLAYED with the stem of her wineglass and avoided looking at Wes directly. "Thanks for dinner. It was great."

Beneath the table at their corner booth, his hand slid up her thigh. "You're welcome."

Her whole body tingled. After nearly having sex in her office—only interrupted by a brisk knock on the door by one of the firefighters trying to get a count for dinner that night—she'd vowed to find some restraint. She wasn't some silly teenager, hip-deep in her first intimate relationship. She was an adult and a professional. She was an empowered woman who didn't need a man to fulfill her life.

Her conscience yawned.

Her libido held up a protest sign. *I want Wes!*

Great. Her own body was against her.

"I'm not going to attack you in the middle of the restaurant, you know." The seductive, spicy scent of his cologne washed over her as he leaned toward her. "But later..."

Her conscience woke up.

Her libido found a new sign—*Yessss!*

"We can pretend to discuss the case," he continued. "At least until I get you out of here."

"Anything else?" the waitress asked upon her sudden appearance.

Wes smiled at the waitress, while his hand crawled to the heat between Cara's legs. "We're great. Thanks."

The waitress cleared the plates, and Cara noticed she'd eaten little. She'd been starved earlier, and the grilled chicken pasta had sounded great. But that was before she'd sat so close to Wes, before she'd smelled him and felt the thrill of his smile. She couldn't concentrate on anything but him.

And Wes had sliced through a two-inch steak without any problem.

Time was critical in this case. Their arsonist had torched two buildings in less than two weeks. Tomorrow would mark the one-week anniversary of the last fire. When would he strike again?

And all she could think about was how much she loved Wes. It was crazy.

She wasn't exactly sure when it had all happened. Sometime between his first cocky smile and the moment she'd realized he wanted so much to belong, yet felt so distant from everyone. Somewhere between his irrational suspicion of Addison, and his need to right the wrongs for so many. Somewhere between the initial heat of lust in his eyes and the tenderness of his touch…she'd found the love of her life.

And she had no idea how to deal with any of it.

They lived in different cities. They'd agreed to a temporary fling. Their careers were top priorities. And who knew how he felt about her? It could never work.

"I'll still respect you in the morning, Captain."

Her gaze shot to his. "You will, huh?"

"Oh, yeah." His finger flicked across her femininity, and even through her jeans the intimacy of his touch shot her desire off like a rocket. "You can relax." His thumb pressed against the seam. "In fact, please do."

Before she could think to control her response, her muscles loosened, then tightened in anticipation of his next stroke. She was shocked to find tears stinging her eyes. She looked down, hoping he wouldn't notice. "We shouldn't be—"

"Hi, guys."

Cara swallowed frantically, then glanced up to see Skyler and a very tall, very gorgeous man standing in front of the table.

"Hey, Sky, Jack. Join us," Wes said, extending his hand to the right side of the booth, scooting closer to Cara to make more room.

Noticing her luscious lieutenant took this opportunity to plaster himself alongside her body, Cara couldn't exactly complain.

Skyler's hunky companion leaned around his wife. "I don't think we've met, *cher.* I'm Jack."

Blinking at the accent—at the sheer, raw magnetism of his presence—Cara leaned forward to shake Jack's hand. "Cara Hughes."

Wes squeezed her thigh. "Cara's here to investigate the arsons."

"And you're making progress?" Jack asked.

Cara glanced at Wes. Progress at overwhelming desire? *Check.* Progress at confusion? *Check.* Progress at prosecution? *Uh…sorta.* "We're still accumulating evidence."

"Suspects?" Jack asked.

Somehow finding the arson investigator that still existed within her, Cara smiled politely. "We're still accumulating evidence."

Jack's gaze slid to his wife, then back to Cara. "This is family, *cher.* I'm not sellin' my story to CNN."

Cara wasn't used to sharing her cases with so many people, but she acknowledged that she probably sounded hard and difficult. "We've got a few leads, but we have little concrete evidence."

Skyler scowled. "What's holding things up? I, for one, don't want to see my husband fighting another one of those fires."

Jack slid his hand over his wife's. The look on his face was one of such adoration it took Cara's breath away. Wow. What would she do if a man looked at her like that? If *Wes* looked at her like that?

Probably fall to my knees at his feet and yell, "Screw my career!"

It was the fear of that level of vulnerability that had forced her to hold back on relationships in the past. Would her love for Wes lead to that kind of trust? She'd shared emotions and thoughts with him that she'd never thought she would. Could there be even more?

"I'm sure Cara and her team are doing the best they can," Jack said, bringing Cara from her thoughts.

She met Skyler's gaze. "We're dealing with a prominent—and controversial—citizen. I'd rather keep our progress quiet until we have more evidence."

Jack nodded. "Understood."

Maybe a fresh telling of the facts would help. Maybe Jack and Skyler could make some sense of the case that had escaped her normally quick mind. So, she ran down the evidence they had, including Addison's gambling debts, the missing glove and the possibility that a cop was involved.

"I can't imagine anybody at the station who'd go so far to help an arsonist," Jack said, his eyes narrowed.

"It makes all this even more terrible," Skyler added.

"So, I guess you think Addison's guilty," Jack said.

Wes's fingers again flexed around Cara's thigh. "We're staying neutral."

Jack and Skyler exchanged a look. "*You* are?"

For Wes's benefit, Cara ignored the teasing. "Addison is our best suspect."

"You know," Jack said, "for all your reluctance to tell us that, you sure didn't hold back to the press the other day."

Cara held Jack's gaze unflinchingly. "I didn't say anything about Addison being a suspect."

"Something along the lines of not eliminating him, I believe, was what you said."

Clearly there was a brain behind Big Jack's brawny body. "Uh-huh."

"And Addison has certainly had a busy few days in the press. Can't turn on the news without seeing something about him. With all that pressure, who knows what he might do?"

Cara smiled. "Who knows."

CARA PRESSED harder on the gas pedal. If she didn't hit much traffic going through town, she might find Wes still at the station. She'd been up since just after five, but she'd never felt less tired. They'd been apart most of the day, and she couldn't wait to see him. She could collapse later—in his arms.

The night together and the day apart hadn't helped her figure out what to do about their relationship. She sensed Wes cared about her, but she also sensed some distance. If she told him about her feelings would he smile? Or run? How could they balance any kind of relationship? Between two different cities? Two demanding careers?

Red and blue police lights suddenly reflected off her rearview mirror. She glanced at her speedometer. Okay, maybe she'd pushed it.

Well, hell. She didn't have time for this. Maybe she'd know the cop, and he'd let her off without too much hassle.

She pulled her car onto a side road and was out of the car with her investigator's ID held high in one hand before the officer had brought his car to a full stop. Blinded by his headlights, she only saw the form of a uniformed man walk toward her. She shivered in the brisk wind and took a second to glance at the passenger's seat, where she'd left her leather jacket during the drive up from Atlanta.

"Good evening, officer. My name's Cara—"

She stopped when she recognized the guy. Eric Norcutt. Great. As she recalled, she'd been kind of bitchy to him the last time she'd seen him.

"Eric, right?"

He angled his head. "Captain Hughes. Going a little fast, weren't you?"

She winced. "Yeah. Sorry about that. I've been working in Atlanta all day. I was anxious to get back."

He stepped closer, almost uncomfortably close. Only pride kept her from scooting back. "The sheriff has us really crackin' down on speeders."

"I bet," she said casually, though she couldn't help a stab of annoyance. Most cops didn't bother the fire department. "Look, if you have to give me a ticket, let's get on with it. I really need to—"

She never even had time to scream as he brought his nightstick down across the back of her neck.

WES STOPPED beside David Hammond's desk. "Can I talk to you?"

"You are."

"How about my office?"

Hammond looked up, his gaze meeting Wes's. "Look, Kimball, I've had a lousy week, and I don't feel like—"

"It's about your wife."

Hammond glanced around, but nobody was paying any attention to them. Then he rose without a word. Wes led the way down the hall to his office. Once they were seated, he didn't hesitate in getting to the point. "How long have you known about the affair?"

"As long as it's been going on—a couple months."

"You realize this gives you a motive for these arsons."

Hammond clenched his fists. "Yes."

"Did you set the fires?"

"Hell, no!" Hammond rose and paced the length of the office. "This is my problem, mine and my family's. Of course I hate Addison, but I want to beat the crap out of him, rearrange his pretty face. I wouldn't go to the trouble to set a bunch of fires, and I sure as hell wouldn't drag my buddies out of bed to deal with my mistakes."

Wes leaned forward, bracing his forearms on his desk. He was very afraid somebody else out there, somebody they both knew, didn't feel that way. At least his gut had been right about Hammond. "Why are you moonlighting for him?"

He shrugged. "I wanted to see what he's like. He didn't realize I knew. I'm sure it gave him some kind of sick pleasure to hire me."

"There's a chance all this is going to get dragged into court at some point. You might want to keep that in mind."

Hammond headed for the door. "Yeah. I figured."

"I'm sorry, man."

"Yeah. Me, too."

Wes turned his attention back to the pile of paperwork that had gathered on his desk over the past week. What would he do if the woman he loved cheated on him? He'd do exactly what Hammond was doing—blame himself. Wonder what he could have done differently.

He looked up as his brother strode into his office. Wes had to remind himself to chill, since he'd expected Cara and his heart rate had quickened accordingly.

Ben dropped into the chair on the other side of his desk. "Want to get a beer?"

Wes glanced at his watch. "I'm waiting for Cara to get back."

Smiling, Ben nodded. "Things getting pretty serious between you two?"

Wes had no idea. Things felt serious—at least to him. But he and Cara had established rules. No one-night stand. No forever. *The duration of the case.* Cara liked rules. He doubted she'd appreciate him trying to change them.

But, dammit, he didn't want her to leave.

"You love her, don't you?"

Wes's gaze shot to Ben's. "Maybe."

"Maybe? You either do or you don't."

"How do you know?"

Ben rose, looking way too amused. "You'll know when you know."

Wes threw up his hands. "Oh, *that's* helpful." The fact that Ben had come into his office last spring with the same doubts and confusion now raging through Wes made him want to throw something. He hadn't asked for Cara to come into his life. He hadn't expected to be blown away by her eyes, her intelligence, her single-minded dedication to her job. And now he couldn't imagine his life without her.

Holy hell, maybe he really was in—

"Wes, we need to talk," the mayor said as he waddled inside the office.

"Now?" Wes asked with another frustrated glance at his watch.

"You, too, Ben. Have a seat." The mayor extended his hand to a chair, then shut the office door.

Most of the time Wes considered the mayor a minor annoyance, and occasionally an embarrassment, but he was always dedicated to his job and to Baxter. Something was very wrong, and Wes had a moment of regret that he'd been the cause.

The mayor paced beside his desk. "I understand you have a personal grudge against Mr. Addison."

Wes watched the polyester bell bottoms on the

mayor's pants as they flapped against his short legs and said nothing.

"Your girlfriend preferred him to you," the mayor went on.

Wes ignored the dig and met Ben's gaze. His brother certainly hadn't brought this up to the mayor. So who had?

"I didn't say anything," Ben said.

"I never thought—"

The mayor wrung his hands. "Well, that answers my other question. You knew about this, Ben? You allowed him to investigate this case anyway?"

Wes kept his attention on his brother. Had their relationship deteriorated so much that Ben questioned their level of trust? What had he done? How had he let things get this bad?

"This is going to be in the papers," the mayor continued. "And not just here. Those Atlanta reporters have been hanging around all week. What if the AP picks up the story? What if the *National Enquirer* shows up at my office?"

Ben sighed. "Calm down, Mayor. The fact that Wes and Addison once dated the same woman isn't ideal, of course. But that's one of the reasons I brought in Captain Hughes. She's made the decisions in the investigation. Her reputation is impeccable." His gaze slid briefly to Wes's, and Wes knew he was thinking about with whom Cara had spent the past several nights. That coming to light on the heels of the connection with Addison wouldn't be good for anyone. If he blew this case for his brother, Cara or the town, he'd never forgive himself.

But he wouldn't let that happen, and he found the timing of this gossip very interesting. "I'm curious how you came about this information about my personal life," Wes asked Mayor Collins.

"There was an anonymous tip called in to my office," he returned defensively.

Wes crossed his arms over his chest. "An anonymous tip? Just as we're about to break this case. That's convenient."

"Is it true?" the mayor countered. "Do you have a personal grudge against Mr. Addison?"

Wes rose and faced the man who could fire him with a snap of his fingers. He valued his job as nothing else. But the time had come to trust his own instincts, to believe in himself. He was right. He'd been right all along.

"I don't like Robert Addison, but not because of a woman. I think he's dishonest, a manipulator and guilty of these arsons."

He glanced at Ben, whose eyes widened, then he directed his attention back to the mayor.

His face had turned orange.

"You'd better have some proof to back up that accusation, Lieutenant."

He had the IOU and the fingerprints, but since he didn't entirely trust the mayor—or his friends—he had no intention of saying anything. "I'll get proof."

The mayor planted his hands on his hips. He stared Wes down, which was difficult to do, since the man was a good five inches shorter. "I need results."

"You'll get them. We just need a little more time."

The mayor sighed. "I'm getting lots of questions

about this. People doubt my judgment in letting you work on this case."

"*I* put him on this case," Ben pointed out.

"And I'm supposed to watch over you." The mayor's hound-dog eyes drooped. "I'm ultimately responsible for this town."

Ridiculously, Wes felt his protective instincts rise. Robert Addison was a pain in the ass to everybody. As soon as he arrested the jerk, he didn't see how he was going to resist punching him straight in the mouth.

"And who's questioning you?" Wes asked. "Addison?"

The mayor stared at his feet. "Not directly."

"But he's behind it."

"Maybe."

Maybe was something. More support than Wes had ever gotten from the mayor. He had the sense to be grateful. "You'll let us finish this?"

"Keep me updated," the mayor mumbled, then turned and strode from the office.

When the door closed behind him, Ben said, "Poor guy. He's watching probably his biggest campaign contributor go up in smoke."

Wes angled his head. "Was that a joke? It wasn't funny."

Ben sank into a chair. "I thought it was hilarious." He paused. "Why are we always at each other's throats?"

Wes leaned back against his desk. "The case has everybody on edge."

"It's more than that, and you know it."

His heart pounding, Wes said nothing for a moment, then he met Ben's gaze. "You don't have to apologize for me."

"I worry about you."

"You don't have to be Dad."

Ben's face flushed. "Somebody had to be."

And it simply came down to that—responsibility versus irresponsibility. Doing what was right and proper versus doing what you wanted and to hell with the rest of the world.

As he had the other night, Wes let himself think about those weeks and months after his father's death. The overwhelming grief and sense that the world had come to an end. At least his world. He'd pulled inside himself. Withdrawn from his family, from his friends. He'd been an angry and resentful twelve-year-old, a handful for his delicate mother's psyche.

He also allowed himself to remember how Ben had stood up under the pressure, had really taken over as the man of the house. He'd resented that leadership. Had somehow known that was what their father had expected of Ben.

But what had Dad expected of him?

He hadn't known then. He didn't know now.

"Does everybody expect the worst of me, so that's why I rebel? Or do I rebel because everybody expects the worst of me?"

"I'm not quite sure I followed that, but I know I don't expect the worst of you."

Wes raised his eyebrows.

"*All* the time."

Glaring, Wes leaned forward. "I resent your authority."

Ben glared back. "I resent your freedom to resist authority."

"Do you want to take me off this case?"

"Hell, no."

The tension drained out of Wes. There was nobody who could piss him off quicker than Ben, but there was nobody whose respect he wanted more. The arsons were the biggest crisis Baxter had seen in many years. If Ben thought for a second that he couldn't do the job, he would pull him. His sense of community was too great.

But if Ben believed in him, then that was all Wes needed to make everything else work. "Are we going to punch each other or hug now?"

Ben blinked. "We could hug."

They did—though in a brief, manly way—then Ben stepped back. "Okay, so you want to bring me up to speed on the case?"

"Cara and I found out some important evidence over the weekend." Wes explained the call from George and his IOUs—proof that Addison had big debts. "I've been trying to keep an open mind—mainly because Cara asked me to—but this information, plus something odd I heard during my interviews with other cops, has convinced me I was right from the start. Addison is behind the arsons. I *know* it."

Ben trailed his hand through his hair. "What happened in the interviews?"

"I think Eric Norcutt may have something to do with all this."

Ben stiffened. "How?"

"He mentioned something about Vegas a few days

ago, and when the proof of Addison's gambling debts came to light, I remembered that. A lot of people gamble, I guess, but then when I was interviewing all the cops about the missing glove, he denied ever going to Vegas. And when I asked him about Addison specifically, he jumped to blame him. Said he probably set the fires for the insurance money."

"Didn't a lot of people think Addison was guilty?"

"A few, but they kind of danced around it. Like they know he's a prominent citizen and didn't want to piss anybody off. Eric didn't hesitate. He was defiant about his accusation."

Again, Wes ran through the details in his mind. He wished he could make things work out so Eric didn't fit. "*Somebody* stole that glove. The evidence points to someone on the inside. I didn't want to believe it, because I thought we were friends, but then this morning I remembered something else. The day Cara and I interviewed Addison, Eric was going into his office as we were coming out. He's moonlighting as a guard, and that's too many coincidences for me. There's no proof in any of this, of course, but I have this feeling..."

Ben didn't argue that feeling. In fact, he said nothing at all.

Wes glanced at him. His brother's face was pale.

"Eric came by the station earlier. He asked casually about Cara—where she was, what she was doing, how the investigation was coming."

Wes's heart actually stopped. "What did you say?"

"I told him she'd been to Atlanta, that she was expected by early evening."

Wes didn't think, he was nearly sure he didn't

breathe. He snagged his jacket off the back of his chair, even as he punched her number into his cell phone. "We have to find her."

"I'm right behind you."

"Was Norcutt in uniform when you saw him?"

"Yeah, but he said he was headed home."

After jumping into Wes's truck, they skidded out of the police station parking lot, Wes continuing to dial her cell number, though he just kept getting her voice mail.

His heart raced; his pulse pounded. She always carried her phone. Where was she? Why didn't she answer?

The possibilities that rolled through his mind were unacceptable. She was a resourceful woman. If Eric or Addison approached her, she'd be on guard. She was armed, experienced and smart as hell.

Beneath these rationalizations, though, guilt pulsed through his body. He should have told her about Eric. He'd hesitated yesterday. For once, he'd resisted his instincts. He'd wanted to wait for proof. If that mistake cost him…

"She's fine," Ben said, clutching the door handle as Wes screeched around a corner. "She's resourceful. She's smart. She's armed. Have you ever seen her without that pistol?"

He had, actually, but he assumed Eric Norcutt wouldn't get that far. But the idea of anybody else touching her had him pressing even harder on the gas pedal.

They screeched into the parking lot of Eric's building. Wes had picked him up a couple of times when they'd gone out to the bars, so he knew which apartment he lived in, but he didn't really have a plan beyond pounding on his door. While his brain buzzed with worry and anger, he forced himself to think like a cop and think of Eric as a suspect.

Eric was aggressive at times, had an attitude about authority, but then someone Wes knew very well could be described exactly like that. Though lately—and in hindsight—he realized Eric had been unusually lax about his job. Late for shifts, his attitude less than enthusiastic, especially last month, when all that had been required was solving a slightly overheated dispute between opposing football fans at a local bar.

He'd been cockier than usual, too. Maybe because now he felt he had friends in high places?

Wes and Ben slid to a stop in front of the door at the same time.

Wes pounded. "Eric, you there?"

Nothing.

He pounded again. "Come on, man. It's important."

No one came.

He glanced briefly at Ben. He wasn't sure they had a right—or even probable cause. If they found any evidence during an illegal search, it wouldn't be admissible in court. Unless… "I think Eric may be in danger, Chief. We should force our way inside, just to be sure."

Wes half expected his brother to balk, but he simply nodded. "I agree, Lieutenant."

Wes slid his pistol from his holster, then tucked his brother behind him and fired at the lock. They busted through the door together. The apartment was garishly decorated in leopard prints and black leather, casually messy—clothes on the floor, dirty dishes in the sink—and empty of its occupant.

Wes took the kitchen, while Ben rushed back to the bedroom. Wes yanked open drawers and cabinets, flipped through stacks of receipts, take-out menus and crumpled business cards.

"Found something," Ben called from the bedroom.

They met in the bedroom doorway, and Ben handed Wes a clamped together stack of small receipts. "Gambling markers. No wonder he and Addison became such buddies."

"And this." Ben gave him a business card.

Glancing at the card, Wes sighed. "He's a bookie. Baxter PD brought him in last year on suspicion of assault, but he was never charged. The witness recanted." He glanced around the room. All this might help at some point, but it wasn't helping him find Cara. "Let's keep looking."

Ben started on the closet, and Wes took the dresser. Beneath a stack of T-shirts, he found blueprints of several of Addison's properties. Three, in fact. Two had already been torched by the arsonist, and the last was a warehouse off the lake road.

"I found a box of latex gloves in the closet," Ben said.

Wes continued to stare unblinkingly at the plans. At what had to be the next target. His hands tingled. His head throbbed. "No kidding? That's convenient."

"Convenient?" Ben approached him. "What did you find?" He paused, then drew in a swift breath, obviously noticing the plans. "Dammit. Those are the layouts of the arson sites."

"Yep."

"This whole thing stinks to high heaven. For a guy nobody suspected until an hour ago, Eric Norcutt is awfully careless. Why—"

"I don't give a rat's ass about Eric." He held up the drawing of the warehouse that had yet to be targeted. "I want to know where this place is. It looks like it's near your house."

Ben glanced over the plan. "The address is near—" He stopped, his gaze connecting with Wes's. "This is the next arson location."

Wes fought against the panic smothering his chest. He silently chanted Cara's name. Maybe if he kept her constantly in his thoughts, she'd stay safe. "Get me there."

11

INVOLUNTARILY, Cara's shoulders jerked, protesting their unnatural position as the rope binding her hands was retied around the steel pole behind her. Her head hurt like hell. Her heart pounded at an irregular pace. She felt sick to her stomach. Her mind, though, was dead calm.

"Let's make sure these knots are nice and tight," Robert Addison said in her ear as he knelt next to her, his warm breath brushing her nape. "It wasn't very nice of you to sic those reporters on me."

She resisted the urge to glare at both him and his junior partner, and closed her eyes as another wave of nausea washed over her. Waking up in the trunk of a squad car hadn't been on her agenda for the night. Eric had probably given her a concussion to go with her hefty dose of humble pie. She'd never taken him seriously as a suspect in any of this. Maybe because he and Wes seemed kind of chummy. Maybe because her focus had been on her libido instead of her case.

She was getting her ass out of here in one piece just so she could kick the crap out of Addison, Eric *and* the irresistible lieutenant.

She thought about the night Wes had tied her up.

The feeling of being overwhelmed, trapped, helpless—the very emotions trying to bubble up inside her now. With Wes, she hadn't mourned the loss of control for more than a moment. Here, she wanted to explode with frustration.

Addison slid his gloved hand down her leg. She fought the urge to shudder. "You shouldn't be here at all," he said, rising to stare down at her. "If you want to blame someone, blame Ben Kimball."

Furious she'd allowed Eric and this idiot to get the jump on her, she met his gaze. "Oh, yeah, that's what I'm doing."

"He never should have brought you to Baxter. These losers around here never would have suspected me."

She wanted to dig at him, to point out that Wes had suspected him, but she needed Addison calm until she could escape. Pissing him off would feel good, but it wasn't smart.

"Eric, go get the gas can from my truck."

"Gas?" Eric's gaze swept Cara's position on the warehouse floor. "What for?"

Addison rolled his eyes as if to say, *See what I have to work with?* "To start the fire," Addison said patiently.

Eric retreated several steps. "Hey, man. You just said we were gonna talk some sense into her, maybe knock her around a little. You didn't say anything about killin' anybody."

Addison rose and shrugged. "I'll get it then. And I'll remember your level of commitment the next time I talk to your bookie and tell him I'm through covering your debts."

Eric held up his hands. "All right, I'm gettin' it."

He gave Cara one last glance, then jogged out the warehouse's back door.

I'll remember that, you jerk.

WES PUSHED the truck past ninety.

"We can't help her if we don't get there in one piece," Ben pointed out.

Wes simply tightened his grip on the steering wheel. He couldn't think past the moment he could yank Cara into his arms, the moment he could inhale her flowery scent.

"She's fine," Ben said.

"She'd better be."

"You're completely in love with her, aren't you?"

"Why do you keep asking me that?"

"Aren't you?"

"I'm thinking that's a real possibility."

"You want to talk about it?"

"Not now, no."

His cell phone rang, and he scooped it off the center console, the truck swerving slightly as he pressed the call button. "Kimball."

"Wes, it's Eric."

"Where the hell are you?"

"You need to come to a warehouse on the lake road," he said in a low, strained voice. "1465 Lakeside Street. Hurry. You need to help Cara."

Rage bubbled inside Wes. "Where is she? If you've touched her—"

"She's here. Look, Addison has lost his mind. He's behind the arsons. I…helped him, but I can't…do this."

"Do what?"

"Just hurry."

The line went dead.

KEEPING ADDISON in her sight, and trying to resist the urge to yank at her knots again, Cara slid the tips of her fingers down the back of her jeans and palmed the switchblade she'd pulled from her boot the moment she'd regained consciousness. Eric had made the mistake of binding her hands in front of her, rather than behind, when he'd dumped her into his truck. That decision, plus the wardrobe choice she'd made to put on her worn boots—with the knife sheathed inside—may have just saved her life.

Addison crouched in front of her again. "I'm really sorry about this, Cara. You're quite lovely, but you've become a problem." He angled his head. "I didn't think you were going to be that day you came to my office. But then I saw you on the news…."

Yet another reason to hate the damn press.

Addison brushed a strand of hair off her forehead. "It's really a shame."

Cara jerked her head back. Okay, maybe pissed off was fine. She'd rather he hit her than stroke her. And she needed to keep him talking and distracted until she could cut herself free. "This won't do you any good, Robbie. I've been working with the police on this. They have all my notes. They'll keep coming after you."

"I doubt that."

"And killing a firefighter is a federal crime. The FBI will be on you. I thought you were smarter than this."

He simply smiled.

God, he really was nuts. How in the world had she

missed the fact that he was a complete, raving lunatic? She'd known he was egocentric, but didn't think he was a clinical narcissist. He was willing to do anything, risk anything, to save his reputation. Next time she spoke to one of the psych guys downtown, she was going to remind them to put "track lighting" in their reports as a key sign.

The back door creaked open, and Eric strode toward them, a large gas can clutched in each hand. He looked pale, but resigned.

As she flicked open the switchblade behind her, she said to him, "You willing to go to the federal pen with your buddy Robbie? That's where you're headed, you know."

Eric's throat moved visibly as he swallowed. "Addison, this is—"

"The only way." Addison rose. "Pour the gas around the perimeter, especially that rotten wood in the corner. Too bad I had to use this empty warehouse. I could have gotten a nice piece of change out of the jewelry store's inventory." He shrugged again. "Oh, well. This place is insured all the same. And the privacy was necessary."

As her hands tingled from lack of circulation and from the effort of moving the knife against the ropes, Cara absurdly wondered if she was supposed to comment on Robbie the Nutso's diabolical plan. Was he now going to detail every aspect of his crimes? Brag about his criminal and sexual prowess? Probably. Though that would work in her favor.

It was like being in the middle of a bad James Bond movie.

She tightened her sweaty grip on the knife. And

where was one of those cool gadgets like a pen that contains rope-eating acid? Or a—

Suddenly Addison whacked Eric on the back of the head with the butt of his gun.

She blinked. *Oh, damn.* Well, that didn't seem like a good thing.

Her heart raced as she watched Addison drag Eric's unconscious body next to hers, and all the pieces fell into place.

"Eric's going to take the fall for everything," she whispered.

"Very good," Addison commented.

Eric had nabbed her, he'd carried the gas tanks inside, he'd no doubt stolen the missing glove. Addison had obviously found a way to frame him.

"What about his motive?" she asked quickly, reluctantly hiding the blade in her hand as Addison moved closer. If she was next on his list of people to whack with that gun, her big escape plan was going to flop. "What does Eric have to gain by setting the fires?"

"Poor Eric. He has a gambling problem, you know. I loaned him money so many times," Addison said with a sad shake of his head. "But it just wasn't enough, obviously. He was so angry with me. Came to my office the other day and threatened me."

The day she and Wes had seen him at Addison's office. "But Officer Hammond was there, too. He'll—"

"Only for a few moments. He left to guard one of my properties."

After which, Addison and Eric had obviously held a meeting about the fires. Addison was going to twist everything to make himself the victim.

"He knew you were on to him, had to get rid of you. He set the fire, but he didn't expect you to fight him. You managed to kick him, knock him off his feet." He sighed. "Tragically, he hit his head. And with you tied up…well, neither of you survived."

He smiled that calm smile again. "You *are* a martial arts expert, aren't you?"

Her body went cold, and she spent a moment regretting her underestimation of him, as well as Eric. Her confidence in herself, her expertise as an investigator, and maybe even her new confidence as a desirable woman had messed her up in a big way.

She'd always considered herself single-minded. Maybe she really was. She couldn't manage both—personal life and career.

Addison leaned down and ran his finger along her jaw. "I'll send roses to your funeral, Cara. Long-stemmed white ones."

She didn't trust herself to speak and just glared at him. *Creep.* She wasn't dead yet.

His mouth drooped. "I was half hoping you'd beg."

"Keep hoping."

"I feel as though I should be merciful, just the same. I could shoot you, then you wouldn't feel a thing."

With a will she didn't know she had, she kept her voice calm when she said, "But that doesn't work with your scenario."

Somehow cocky and regretful, he patted her cheek and stood. "No, I guess not. Don't be sad, though. The smoke will probably choke you before the flames get you."

"Gee, that's encouraging."

DROPPING THE PHONE on the console, trembling with rage and frustration, Wes briefed his brother on the call.

Ben braced his hand against the dashboard as they made a fast, tight turn. "You were right. About Eric. About Addison."

Wes didn't care about being right. He just wanted Cara safe. Alive and safe.

The phone rang again, and the truck swerved as Wes grabbed for it. But Ben snatched the phone from his hand. "Watch the road. Ben Kimball here," he said into the mouthpiece. "I see," he replied after a moment's pause. "When?" Another pause. "Well, nothing can be done there, I guess."

Wes whipped his head toward his brother. "What happened?"

Ben shook his head impatiently. "Where's the backup Wes called for? We expected to hear sirens behind us by now." Following the charged silence, Ben snapped, "Then move your ass faster." He flipped the phone closed in disgust.

"Dammit, Ben. What happened?"

"They found Cara's car abandoned on a side street just outside of town." He shook his head. "No sign of a struggle. Her gun, her cell phone and her jacket were lying on the passenger's seat. Impressions in the mud indicate another car had pulled in behind her, then left in a hurry. There are fresh, dark tire marks at the edge of the road."

Wes squeezed the steering wheel until he was sure he could pop it in half. "Eric pulled her over in his patrol car, then nabbed her."

"Likely. She wouldn't have seen him as a threat until..."

A stab of pain and despair punched into his stomach. "Until it was too late."

SWEAT ROLLED down Cara's face as she tugged on the ropes.

She thought she'd managed to partially cut through the knot, but her fingers were cramping and stinging. She was pretty sure she'd cut herself numerous times, but her hands were so numb she just couldn't feel the sting.

Smoke had filled the warehouse. Flames and heat crept closer, burning her lungs and eyes.

She moved her hand up, then down again, fighting to take shallow breaths and ignore the blinding pain in her head.

Tugging again, she kicked Eric's unconscious body when the ropes didn't so much as budge. "This is all your fault!"

She let her head fall forward, closing her eyes and struggling for calm, for the cool, capable attitude she'd spent so many years cultivating.

It's *your* fault, her conscience whispered. *You* blew this case.

Though her body screamed in agony, and her mind had begun to betray her, she continued sawing on the ropes. Up, then down. She kept her eyes closed. She recalled her training—medical, firearm, firefighter, karate—and let the burning smell of the warehouse, the whispered doubts and the threat of death recede.

And suddenly she was free.

She pushed to her feet, swaying a bit as she stood. Her head spun, her lungs burned. She immediately dropped to a crouch, pressed the button to close the switchblade, then shoved it into her back pocket.

She coughed and blinked through the thick smoke, but she managed to grab Eric's ankle and half-crawl, half-drag them both toward what she thought was the back door. The concrete floor was killing her knees, but the beams creaked and shifted above her, driving her to move faster. Eric's dead weight was heavy as hell, but she didn't dare stop to rest.

A window exploded, and she glanced back, but the smoke had grown so dense, she had only a vague idea where the sound had come from.

She dragged Eric and struggled on, thankfully leaving the worst of the flames behind her. Addison had started the fire far away from the door, so he could make his exit. But this warehouse was obviously old. The main structure might not last long under the onslaught of the gasoline's intense heat.

Just when she thought she couldn't move another foot, she found the door. Laying her palm against it, she nearly cried in relief at the cool touch of steel. She let go of Eric and staggered to her feet, twisting the knob and yanking at the same time.

As freedom and the cool night air rushed across her face, an ominous rumble echoed behind her. Her heart slammed to a halt. A chill skittered down her spine.

She knew that sound. What it meant. What she'd see if she waited a second to turn around.

She reached down for Eric as the building imploded.

FROM SEVERAL BLOCKS AWAY, Wes spotted the flames. With the gas pedal to the floor, all he could do was keep the wheel steady and pray.

"The building's still up," Ben said as they grew closer. "We'll get her out. We won't let anything happen to her."

Wes clamped his teeth together. He wondered how many firefighters had said that to each other over the years. Had his father said the same thing to his team that day so many years ago? How many times had he himself said something similar to calm people down in the middle of a crisis?

But, by damn, he didn't want to feel calm. He wanted to scream and run and pound something.

"Maybe they didn't even bring her here. Maybe Eric lied. Maybe—"

"Shut up, Ben."

As they barreled across the small parking area, he finally heard sirens in the distance. He wouldn't be too late. He'd find her—whole, alive, probably pissed off.

He was leaping from the truck even as he threw the gearshift into park. Not waiting for his brother, he took off at a dead run toward the building.

Then a loud crash ripped through the air.

Seemingly in slow motion, the building collapsed into itself in a pile of ash, flames, wood and steel.

Wes fell to his knees in the grass.

He couldn't move. Or breathe. Or believe.

She couldn't be gone. He refused to let this happen. She'd become the center of his life. In less than a week, he'd finally found someone who understood him completely, without reservation. He couldn't lose her, too.

He stared unblinkingly at the roaring fire for what

seemed like forever, but couldn't have been more than a second or two, since there was no way he was frozen in fear with the woman he loved very likely caught in that burning death trap.

The thought burst through, propelling him to his feet and surging him forward. There had to be a way in. "Cara!" he shouted over the roaring fire. He rounded the building, the heat searing him like a furnace blast.

"Wes! Stop!" Ben yelled from behind him. "We can't do anything until they get here with the hoses."

He ignored his brother and kept running. "Cara!"

As he dashed around the back corner of the building, he saw her.

She was whole. And alive. Dragging a man's body across the grass and away from the building.

He never broke his stride as he streaked toward her, but some part of his totally screwed-up world righted itself. An emotion he barely recognized as pure, blissful happiness pumped through his veins.

Her head lurched up as he reached her. She whispered one word. "Wes."

He yanked her into his arms, holding her against him and glorying in the rapid, but steady beat of her heart. Capturing her mouth with his, he poured fear and passion and relief into his kiss.

He wasn't sure he could ever let her out of his sight again. He'd relive this night way too many times in his nightmares.

"Eric," she mumbled against his lips.

"You forgot me already?"

Pulling back, she smiled. "No, I need to check on him. He probably needs oxygen."

"Let Ben do it."

"No, I—"

Ben rushed past them, then dropped to his knees beside the unconscious man. Practically on his heels, a medic team jogged by, loaded down with equipment.

"He was hit on the back of the head," she called to the medics.

Wes pulled her against him again, pressing his lips against hers and determined not to let any more interruptions distract them. She smelled like smoke, not flowers, but her mouth was warm and alive, and he was sure he'd never need another thing in life but her touch.

When they finally broke apart, she said—though not very convincingly— "We need to go after Addison."

"No chance he's in that burning rubble?"

"Sorry. No."

He was disappointed by that news, but he shrugged. "A Baxter PD team is staking out his house. I even had them call the state police and issue an APB. He won't get away."

"You don't want to go after him?"

He stared into her beautiful aqua eyes. "No. I'd kill him."

Smiling, she started to slide her fingers through his hair. "How did you find—"

He grabbed her bleeding hands. "I'm mauling you, and you need help. Ben!" He swept her into his arms and carried her toward his brother and the other medics.

"Put me down. I'm fine."

"You were in that fire, too. You need oxygen."

"No, I—" She coughed. "I'm fine."

Wes set her gently on the grass and cupped her cheek as Ben knelt next to them to tend to her hands. He must have been blind not to notice before, but her face was dirty, her eyes bloodshot, her clothes torn and filthy. "You don't look fine."

She rolled her eyes. "That's romantic. I almost died, you know."

Wes's own hands shook as he ran them down her arms in search of more injuries. "Don't remind me." He unbuttoned the cuffs of her shirt and rolled up the sleeves. Deep gashes and red marks marred her wrists. Marks that would soon become bruises dotted her forearms.

Nausea and fury welled inside him. "I've changed my mind. I *am* going to kill him."

"I'd rather see his country club-pampered face on the other side of prison bars."

"Can I beat him to a bloody pulp first?"

"I'll see what I can arrange. Now quit being such a mother hen and tell me how you found me."

He quickly told her about his suspicions of Eric, the search of the apartment and finding the blueprints, then Eric's warning call. She told him how Eric had knocked her out, then helped Addison tie her up and arranged the fire until Addison had betrayed him. How she'd cut herself loose with her switchblade and cut her hands in the process.

Wes glanced over at his former friend and colleague. "He must have called when he went outside to get the gas. You could have left him in there. You didn't know he'd tried to help you. You risked your life bringing him out." He met her gaze. "Why?"

"No family should go through what we did," she said simply.

"I love you."

"You— What?"

"You heard me."

Her eyes were wide and just a little fearful. "No, I don't think I did."

His heart was still hammering from the surprise of the words slipping out the first time. He glanced at Ben, who was smiling and doing his best to pretend not to be hanging on every word. "I think I'll check on Eric," he said as he slid away.

Wes stroked Cara's cheek. "I love you."

"You can't. We agreed."

"To keep things simple, to keep things brief and uncomplicated. That just doesn't seem to matter a helluva lot right now."

She shook her head. Her eyes were bright with tears, but her voice held no hesitation. "I'm going back to Atlanta, Wes. I don't belong here. And I can't do this."

He hated all three of those statements and didn't know which one to jump on first. "Can't do what?" he asked finally, searching her face for some semblance of the emotions he felt, some hope that she cared about him at all.

"This. Be with you. Have a relationship. My job is my first priority. I can't do it and be with you, too."

"Why not?"

"I blew it. This case was *my* responsibility. I had no business rolling around with you when I should have been working."

"Are you saying if we hadn't have gotten involved, this case would have turned out differently?"

"Yes!"

Incredulous, he stared at her. "How?"

"Somebody could have gotten killed. Actually, I almost did. I take that very seriously."

"We got the bad guys, Cara. The department is going to call me the moment Addison is in custody. We won."

"That homeless man—"

"His death was a tragedy. But it happened before you even got here." He shook his head. "That excuse won't work."

She rose, her fists clenched at her sides. "I should have suspected Eric."

He stood next to her. "And because you didn't, that's my fault?"

"Yes. If you hadn't come along, looking so gorgeous and irresistible—"

"I'm liking the turn in this argument."

"—I wouldn't have been distracted. I should have focused on my job. I made too many mistakes."

His heart contracted. "And I'm the biggest one."

"Yes. No." She rolled her shoulders. "The mistake would be to continue seeing you. We had a great time together, Wes. Can't we just leave it at that?"

"A great time," he echoed in a hollow voice.

"I have an obligation to the people of this state, to myself, to promises I made when my parents died. I'm committed to my job."

"I was just a great time."

She blinked. Her eyes filled with tears before she looked away. "I can't—"

"Captain Hughes, we're headed to the hospital now," one of the medics said as he approached them.

"Ben says you were hit on the head. We need you to come with us and let the docs check you out." He looked warily from Cara to Wes, as if he expected one—or both—to argue.

"Okay," Cara said, stepping forward.

Wes grabbed her arm. "I'm coming with you."

"No." She wiped the tears from the corners of her eyes, leaned forward and brushed her lips across his cheek. "It was nice working with you, Lieutenant." Then she turned and strode away with the medics.

Wes didn't watch her go. He stood alone and miserable, feeling as though his heart and the building beside him had something in common. They had both collapsed into a pile of broken rubble.

When his phone rang a few minutes later, and the cops told him they'd apprehended Addison, he couldn't have cared less.

12

WES LEANED AGAINST the wall outside Cara's apartment door. He remembered the night he'd first waited for her, with Italian food and a dream to spend the night. They'd come so far since that day. They'd shared more than their bodies and their nights. He hadn't imagined the tenderness in her touch, or in her eyes when she looked at him. He refused to believe all they had together was "a good time."

Actually, you were a *great* time, his conscience graciously reminded him.

"Super. I feel so much better now."

Actually, he felt as if his heart had been ripped from his chest.

I have an obligation to the people of this state, to myself, to promises I made when my parents died. I'm committed to my job.

He'd replayed those words in his head a thousand times since she'd walked away from him. He'd been in shock at the time and hadn't really absorbed their meaning. But now he thought he understood. At least he hoped he did. The thought of her not loving him was almost too much to deal with him, so there had to be something else holding her back.

He'd found a way to accept the tragedy in his life

and move on. He'd even found a new understanding and peace with his brother.

Could he work the same magic with him and Cara?

He had no idea. But he sure as hell was going to try.

When he heard her footsteps on the stairs, he deliberately set his face into a determined expression. She wasn't getting rid of him. He knew she didn't have a concussion, thanks to information from Ben, but she was bruised nearly head to toe. She needed understanding, tenderness. He'd give it all to her, if she only gave him a chance.

She reached the top step with her head bowed.

He fought the need to go to her, to pull her into his arms and soothe her wounded body. He'd do that, but later. He had to find her heart first.

She was two steps away from the door before she hesitated, clearly realizing he was there. But she still didn't look up when she said, "We already said our goodbyes, Wes."

"You did. I didn't."

As she unlocked her door, Cara glanced up at him, at the persistent set of his jaw, the light in his eyes. She didn't have the strength to go another round with him, she really didn't.

How could she push him away when all she wanted to do was crawl in bed and die?

"You can help me pack, I guess."

"You are *not* leaving tonight," he said as he followed her inside.

She somehow found the strength to place her hands on her hips and glare at him. "I'll do anything I please."

"I want you to stay. Tonight. Forever."

Tears burned behind her eyes. Dear God. How could she accept his feelings and still fulfill her promises? Still hold on to the professional she'd made herself into? She was lousy at balancing her personal life and career. Hadn't the last week proved that?

"I can't. I've got to pack." She strode down the hall and into her bedroom.

Naturally, he followed. "Don't pack. Stay. I need you to stay."

She yanked hangers from the closet. "I'm going back to Atlanta, Wes. Back where I belong, doing what I do best."

"You're running."

"I'm leaving."

He grabbed the clothes from her. "If you go, I'm coming with you." He tossed the clothes on the bed and grasped her wrists. "You deserve a life of your own, Cara."

She glared up at him. "I have a life."

"A life aside from long hours at work, arsonists, professional politics and tragedy." He sat on the bed, drawing her down beside him. She decided only her compromised physical state kept her from simply decking him and continuing to pack, but her heart contracted, as if reminding her this man was her one and only, her soul mate, if she could only find the strength to grab onto him, to take a chance on a future full of uncertainty—and, maybe, joy.

"Don't feel guilty about surviving," he said gently. "I used to think the same thing, you know—that my family would have been better off if I'd been taken by the fire, rather than my father."

"It's not just the guilt," she mumbled.

"And I know you want to prevent another tragedy like the one you went through. You want to make a difference. I do, too. You want justice in a world where sometimes there isn't any. I'm right there with you. You want control of your life, authority and respect. You have it.

"I spent a lot of time thinking my job had to be the number one priority in my life," he continued as she tried unsuccessfully to push words past the lump in her throat. "Frankly, I've never met anybody to make me question why that shouldn't be. But I've met that somebody now. You." He slid his thumb across the back of her bandaged hand. "Tell me you don't feel the same way, and I'm out of here. Tell me you don't love me."

She jerked her head up, meeting his gaze. The sharp blue of his eyes seemed more vivid and beautiful than ever. She couldn't tell him that any more than she could resist drawing another breath.

Relief darted through his eyes at her silence. He kissed her forehead. "It's okay to live your life, even though your parents can't."

He understood. She shouldn't have been surprised. If anyone could make sense of her past, he could. She closed her eyes briefly. "I stood over my parents' graves and promised I'd fight for them. I won't compromise that."

He squeezed her hands. "You *have* fought for them. I'm not asking you to give that up. I'll help you keep that promise, in fact. When you need your space, I'll give it to you. When you need help or advice with a case, I'll give it to you. I don't want to rule your life, smother you, or wreck your career. I just want to love you."

She recalled the times he'd supported her, cared for her, loved her body and simply understood her. The tragedies they'd shared. Their teamwork, even when they'd disagreed. Would anyone ever be that close to her again?

No. She loved him and would never love anyone else. But the unknown still hovered before them, a promise and a dark specter rolled into one. "People who love me leave."

"They die."

"Yes."

He pulled her against his side, tucking her head against his neck and shoulder. "I can't promise you that. But I'll never willingly leave you."

She'd been horribly cruel earlier, she realized. All out of fear. "I love you so much I'm afraid of it," she admitted.

He sighed and kissed her forehead. "Finally. I thought I was going to have to nag you for the next fifty years to hear those words."

She punched him lightly in the side. "Pushy, that's what you are." She looked up at him. "We've known each other less than a week."

He raised his eyebrows and glanced at his watch. "Excuse me, Captain, we've known each other exactly one week. It's nearly two, and it's Tuesday."

"It seems much longer."

"Is that a compliment?"

She slid her hand around his neck, pulling his head toward hers, their lips just a breath away from touching. "Absolutely. It takes a lifetime to fall in love, but just a moment to realize it."

When their lips touched, she reveled in his focus,

their closeness, his love for her. They were things she vowed she'd never take for granted. She'd cherish him, and his determination not to give up on her, as long as she lived.

She couldn't touch him long, though, without her body coming to life. Her nerve endings sizzled, her stomach tightened. Despite the long night, her aches and pains, she longed to show him how much he meant to her, to begin fulfilling her promise to their relationship.

Hooking her hand around the back of his neck, she leaned back onto the bed and pulled him on top of her. She slid her other hand to his chest to work the buttons on his shirt.

"What about your bruises?"

She smiled against his lips. "I bet you can be gentle."

He brushed her hair off her face, then drew the back of his hand alongside her neck, beneath the collar of her shirt. "I guess I should apply to the force in Atlanta."

She parted his shirt, running her palms across the breadth of his chest. He was so warm and strong. "Force?" she echoed as his words penetrated her brain. "What for?"

"I'm not settling for a long-distance relationship."

"I could move here."

He pulled back, staring down at her. "You can?"

"Sure. My boss is very flexible."

"One day I think I'm going to be jealous of this relationship between you and the governor."

She slid his shirt off his shoulders, down his arms, then tossed it on the floor. "Okay. Hey, wait a minute. If I move here, do I have to go shopping with Monica and Skyler?"

"Probably."

"Then again, that lingerie shop of Skyler's could come in handy."

He laughed, and she absorbed the wonderful sound deep inside her soul. They'd laugh more in the future, she vowed. She wouldn't let the past bog them down. She wouldn't let the tragedies they shared overwhelm their happiness in finding each other.

She kissed the base of his throat. She really liked that spot. For some reason, his cologne, the essence of his scent, seemed to gather there. She liked the way the rumble of his laughter reverberated through her lips.

But a familiar ringing intruded on her playful mood.

"You've *got* to be kidding," Wes muttered, fumbling in his pocket, then flopping on his side next to Cara. He placed the cell phone next to their ears so they could both hear the call. "Go away," he said into the receiver.

"Have you really arrested Robert Addison?" a sort-of familiar voice asked.

"Who is this?" Wes returned.

"Roland Patterson. Your friendly pet store owner."

Wes rolled his eyes. "How did you get this number?"

Gossip traveled fast in this town, Cara decided. The man had been in custody less than two hours.

Patterson sighed. "Your sis and I are buddies, you know. So, is it true?"

"Yes. Goodbye."

"It's so thrilling to know I contributed to such an important case," Patterson went on as if he hadn't been dismissed.

"You?" Wes's eyes danced as he glanced up at Cara. "How's that?"

"Hmm. Does the name *George* ring a bell?"

Their mysterious informant who didn't really seem to exist? What did Patterson know about that?

"George who?" Wes asked.

"The owner of a few crucial IOUs."

"What do you know about George and IOUs?"

Patterson sighed again. "Darling, who do you think gave him your cell number? Cheerio! I'm off to celebrate."

Wes turned off the phone, closed the case, then shoved it off the end of the bed. "Well, I'll be damned. Roland Patterson helped crack this case."

"You could give him all the credit, then we wouldn't have to talk to any reporters."

Wes kissed her jaw. "That's the second-best idea I've heard all night."

She slid her tongue over his earlobe. "What's the first?"

"Us getting married. And, hey, I know the perfect guy to perform the ceremony."

Married? She swallowed. Though if she was throwing aside her fears, she might as well jump all the way in. "What guy?"

"Well, he might be an unconventional pastor."

"How unconventional?"

He grinned. "In case you didn't know, the mayor is a judge...."